T0114893

MR. RODNEY PAUL WILLIAMS'

A Short Story Series 2

RODNEY PAUL WILLIAMS

authorHOUSE®

AuthorHouse™
1663 Liberty Drive
Bloomington, IN 47403
www.authorhouse.com
Phone: 833-262-8899

Published by AuthorHouse 05/15/2023

ISBN: 979-8-8230-0851-8 (sc)
ISBN: 979-8-8230-0852-5 (e)

Print information available on the last page.

This book is printed on acid-free paper.

CONTENTS

UNLESS I GET A WRITERS JOB

ABOUT THE AUTHOR

My history is in my books, so to all you other authors try this on for size.

I take imaginative liberty.

My mom was Venusian, a Princess. One of her parents four princesses. Oh and there was one uncle too.

My mom was there step-sister.

My Dad, a dethroned king, devoid of family, friends and fortune. I guess my mom took pity on him, so here I am.

Try that on far size.

Mr. Rodney Paul Williams
A.k.a
Rodney Paul Banks

MY ATTEMPT AT WRITING A COWBOY STORY

CHAPTER ONE

He punched Pecos Pete with one punch across the bridge of Pete's nose. Pete had a kind of weird look. Not on his face but in the way being knocked to the dirt street would not have been obvious to ones opinion of how the body reacts when being knocked out.

While still upright and directly after Sam Elliot had used the total of his own body muscles and with a full force landed that right fist, Pete's body went backwards in three hops. Up and down, up and down, up and down, then his body slightly shook and went crash in the dry dirt, blowing up a cloud of dust as he lie there in the street, leaning on his right elbow and forearm, eyes both open but with a glazy I know nothing, I hear nothing, I see nothing, I see nothing expression. Out cold.

The towns people who were on that street got glimpses of what had that to Pecos. Some saw him bouncing, twitch and fall. Some only saw him fall and got a view of his awkward landing and position on the dirt. Fewer son Pecos lying on his side but not getting up. Only two saw the punch being thrown and all that happened afterwards. Those two counted the most, Marshall Bart Bonney and visiting Sheriff James Bowie Crockett.

Sam Elliot confined to his sent a message by Henry nine years old, almost an adult in those days to Lil Dot's pleasure Palace, a two story shack of ill repute, to have Ginger or Mary Anne the Black sent up to his room. Circumstance why he could not come to Lil Dot's he was sure need not be explained. The Marshall frequented the establishment almost every. Speculations were his visits were part of the pay deal for being marshall made with him by all the righteous upstanding citizen including the Mayor Rizzo Franks.

The Jailhouse had become unsuitable as Butch Cassidy gang hand blown the front half of it up with nitro when they Toby Keith, the gangs second in charge and Frank's fastest gun hand was broken out. Two of the thirty man gang were killed both by the marshall. More of the gang could have met Satin, but in the pitch blackness of night innocents who heard the thunderous blast may have gotten inquisitive. The Marshall wanted none of the gangs stray lead to hit any of them.

There get away was made easier because all the gang members rode horses, none of them made use of a camel even though desert surrounder the area by hundreds of miles in either direction.

When the posse of muleskinners, gold miners and a few ranch hands who happened to be spending the night in the Pleasure Palace.

Of the forty one that went twenty six rode unruly tempermental artiodactltia. They were the arch of the problems allowing the total escape of the desperados directly following that problem twenty miles from town the gang disbanded and lit out in various directions leaving trails going in eleven different directions. Four days later the marshall gave in due to the grumpiness of the crumbling posse.

Lil dot had ordered in their absence five new wooden water leak proof sit down in tubs. They were finished being carpentered by the third day of the mens absence. Lil dotty's bath house's wall elaborating the new additions. She only charger five cents more for a hut bath than when the men took up their chase.

On that same day Harvey Weinstein got off the stage coach. Weinstein represented one Joseph Gayetti the founder out medicated paper for the water closet. Weinstein had been traveling cross country telling that toilet paper is now spinter free. The general store took orders for one hundred units. Each unit came in packages of five hundred at sold retail for fifty cents. Drucker's was the general store.

Weinstein gave Sam Drucker a hint at the future telling Sam that in the not too near future mullien is slotted to be sold on a roll. Mullien is the plant medicated paper i.e. toilet paper was made from.

Weinstein mailed back to New York the order for the last twelve general stores one in each town the stage coach line made a stop.

The stage coach was gone by the day the posse returned. None the less Drucker nailed up a wooden sign medicated paper arriving in one month. It really was a big deal. Unspoken yet recorded history was in a meaningful engendering.

CHAPTER TWO

The gang actually did break up. They did not go in different direction, spilt up, to collect together at a later time in a hideaway.

Toby Keith headed towards Canada, Quebec as it is called in this century.

A man was pinned down by a bush wacker. Keith analyzed the situation called out to the ambusher's surrender and if you wish not to surrender, retreat and leave be that traveler. A bullet from the would be ambuster came towards Keith's direction twenty feet away. Are you an asshole or just can't shoot? He thought to himself more maybe he just wants to tell me mind my own trail. Keith stood from behind the boulder. Another shot came Keith's way and knicked his shoulder. Like the time it takes darkness disappearing when lightning flashes Keith drew. The ambusher's gut burned hot. The back bone shattered.

Keith was thanked by Thomas Master son. Come on into Iberville for a café dinner and a shot of red eye. I would invite to the house but I am on my from our Senator's office. I am hurried Cate, Uh Catherine is due soon. The two road into the city. The sign said, Iberville country, Quebec Canada. That same day Bartholemew William Barclay Masterson was issued into this world a healthy bouncing baby boy born to bear a Canadian hero in the United States of America.

Sometime in the next few days Rexaford Harrison's corpse was being bitten into pieces by coyote and wolves. Ambushers it seems need no funeral nor recognition what they left would stink to high heavens and maggots would clean away the rot down to skeletal bones.

At the leaf Resterante, their steaks were to order and Masterson to himself mused tender as Cate's bottom.

Talk managed its way to why Keith had traveled unless I am in an displeasing order. Came to a good Legal piece. Got an outstanding warrant for my arrest down south. Knifed a guy. Fair fight. Gang I used to be in outlaws broke out be my trial. Here tell I might have own. I don't like running being a free is more of my lifestyle. Running from the law dogs down south usually don't give one a cotton to.

The three adults and baby became unseperable. When the husband and wife went to America. Keith rode along as body guard, bouncer for baby bat on Keith knee, teacher to father and mother on gun toting and gun use. The Masterson's taught an illiterate how to decipher these squiggley symbols on letters, newspapers and books into sensible usages.

Keith read a lot. The Masterson's bed a lot and bat Masterson until age two peed a lot in him diapers.

Keith had every lawbook in every town the four passed through as though they were nomadio. Keith mostly read law. Self defense. A couple on himself and his former gang. His picture in the book gave accredation to the writer, big bob Thornton, who got Keith's image damn near perfect.

Big bob Thornton in addition to being a highly published author ran a hugely successful explosives business. Toby to himself enamoured Thornton. Not bad for a jailbreak expert.

In New York Keith discovered the precedent to make him a wanted outlaw no longer. He filed papers. Six months later while Thomas had attended a very important business meeting which would move he and his family to Illinois, Catherine put bat to sleep and gave Keith a long loving farewell. Keith left that day before Thomas returned. He left a note Thomas would comment. Cate took him to bed as Bartholomew began to arouse into wide-eyed awakening and a hunger for a teet or two. Thomas soothed his loving greatful wife as Bart suckled.

CHAPTER THREE

Twenty years later.

The branch was a goody sturdy at least a foot and a half around and full of sap as was tree. It would both of their weights well. He was hung first. While he still twitched his boots were doused with the lamp oil from Miss Curth's own bedroom lamp.

The deputy hit him in his knees with a club then set his boots ablaze. He was still twitching as the fire caught.

The towns crude rough neck explained to his good friend of thirteen years.

I taint uh never seen nor nor heard uh such a thang in my whole plumb life. To see uh hanging feller in such pain and misery anna tryin to holluh whilest the rope was a gaggin om to silence. Depty's just one mean ole varmint. He did his is job mind yuh. But he's a meanun.

Marshul should I eva girl in that ninevh trouble anna he comes a after me umma guna has tuh gun im, gun im dade.

Report given as the marshal had depotized him for two weeks to back deputy Alex Cord. His back as far as gun play-well none other than, Marshall Marian M Wayne, could hope to match his quickness, accurateness and fairness. Deputy Alex Cord could not come close to either in gun play, but he was no run of the mill six gun totter either.

The next morning Marshall Wayne called together the people at the hanging. He needed to determine since the judge had not come to town, did the citizens have a hanging on a lyching. Before he wired the territorial Rongers assigned to this vast area all his questions most be answered and verified. He was the honest killer who was looking towards this governorship. The meeting took place in the restaurant over breakfast but one at a time.

The testimony all stood aligned. He gave it a judgement of a legal but brutal execution.

The train rolled into the station and well dressed Cananian migrating from Illhois got off, headed to the stable car. His favorite and loyal steed Betty white had already been saddled and was parading down the wooden ramp. The stable hand was now feeding a fresh Golden Delicious. She had finished off the bunch of sweet orange carrots just as the train had stopped.

The sign on the station read Welcome All Law Abidina Peoples to Dodge City Province.

Glob Goblonski, Mayor- Marion M. Wayne Marshall- Wyatt Earp Business Administration CEO. In smaller letters read, stay out of trouble while you're in this town. We hang varments, horse and cattle thieves and you if you commit any other hangin offense.

Four later Wyatt Earp, Bat Masterson, Marion M. Wayne took a picture together. The four were standing by an open coffin. Conwyn Connie Carlin was inside. The nine bullet hole and bloody shirt still on him.

Three years before the four of them walker into a bar in Tombstone to arrest or rest him in peace. Carlin made his last maniacal jesture believing his own hype as the greatest gunslinger that had ever lived. He slapped leather.

They came in from three different cities at the request of Wayne. Met outside the city until all our rode in.

Carlin had gone one on one against Dodge's crude roughneck. Carlin walked away from the fair fight. Carlin did not walk away from this one. Marshall Wayne justified the warrant for Carlin's arrest because showdowns were forbidden dodge.

None of the other three would ever mention the Marshall Wayne did not Carlin alone. The reasoning was should one of the others ever need the same just a fiable favor.

The photographer decided after hearing how Carlin got it never took any of the for again refusing to do Wyatt's brothers wedding. His excuse, it is a horrid time to exit Dodge. Business here is too good. The school mam came up with a great idea. Photograph her full wedding. She talked all parents into having each of the school kids picture at graduation.

While that discussion was talking place and odor wafted the air. In the times when medicine paper on a role of cardhorg the Marshal's wife had just wiped her butt hole in the toilet room.

Her hastiness led to her forgetting to close the window. She used her perform on her dress, inside by butt and outside where she sat down. She had noticed in church how some of the other women smelled of fecal matter as they walked past her and some others were perfumed. She got the message.

Phem Mihn had the best lunchonet in the city. Not a day went by when someone influential enjoyed and unaccustomed dimsum, roasted park, beef and vegetables, chicken fried, roasted and sheddred. She also had for the Santa Fe, an old European custom sandwiches for take out. Take out. How ingenious for the time.

Mayor's, Governors, business investors and twice the vice president of the United States doing speculations for further western political business mouth's had be napkined sue to her cooks traveling cuisine.

Marshall and Misses Wayne made another thing the Lunchonet's proprietor made use of, reservations to meet there today. Their wedding anniversary. The ninth.

The reception area held at every opening until after closing one Bruce Li Jun-Fen clad in Cantonese formal wear. Most polite human one would wish to meet. You would even think that this short five feet, thin one hundred eleven pounder with good facial features was as deadly with his body as most of the elitist fast guns.

He never had to use them, the law in Dodge had earned a well reknown reputation both east and west. Should the opportunity had presented itself, a armed man, two, three, four incited distemperature at a distance his hands and feet would not stop a bullet he had personally hand carved ten wooden darts. No more need be written on the matter. In the country of China he was of greatest recognition in his arts of combat.

Li Jun Fen at his post near the front entrance always alert and always aware of the surroundings raised an eyebrow what a squadron of Calvery passed by on the other side of the avenue. They were information. This meant they were hare on orders. Orders meant army business. In front of them was a very famous mule skinner and scout. From their constant movement, there were headed towards the Indians camping ground Jun-Fen had not been in the sates long, only two years, so he was with personal experience unware the Indians once almost as the bison, numbers as were the bison thinning out and fast.

As the train owners had the bison killed off to rot away and to cut the Indian food supply completely off, thus the second major maneuver to conquer and obtain the land.

The Calvery Captain did not believe what was before his eyes Corporal Vargas, peck the bones the wagon. Take four troops with you and get that skeleton back to Colonal Graff. Give the colonal this post. Get it done now.

Vargas took O'Rourk, Donnelly and Sparks Jethro along with his brother two years younger at nineteen Sparks John Samuel. He did as he was told the post he never asked what was in it, nor did he open it.

Colonal. Graff did not want to believe what he saw even though the report of the fifteen feet skeleton's why he sent Captain Custer and the squad to investigate the report. He only Custer, take a squad to Chief Thomas and report back on what he tells and shows you. One more thing Custer the colonal broached. Should you be astonished have a report sent back to me immediately with proof of your new awareness.

Custer had awaited along with the rest of his squad. A requested guest of Chief Thomas.

The giant skeletal remains garotted his attention so porely he never even considered the the skeletons of camels buried there with the skeleton of a five foot ten human skeleton the reminds of a hindu camel driver imported to the west to train and handle the tempermental camels cowboys, muleskinners and miners had no idea how to.

It is not permitted to indulge your appetite as to how those common people ever lerned of the foreigners existence and skill of camel training or a long lost US governmental plan on how to excise the Indian territories would come light. How the camel jockey somehow landed in America from their own continent on the other side of the planet? Chief Thomas had ceased digging until the calvery response he had sent for arrived.

Custer along with Thomas ordered the digging to continue. The chief's warriors sought the advise and when given the ritual of sage to carry off evil from them disturbing the burial ground. The tribal Medicine Man Blique would not give protection to his white enemy, the Long Knives, so Custer kept his troops distanced.

CHAPTER FOUR

Isider and Nellie walked into a lousy street. People passing by on either side of the one of the most beautifully shrubbed and treed area in the city. The citizenry who had not been invited took notice gave approving glances and nods. A congratulator wave came from an old female. Walking with who could have been husband for four or five decades. The spouse crossed to the wedding party and inquired who is the best man. Found him and said are you the one who talked the groom into this, uh, uh, celebration for the death of his bachelor hood?

The bride and groom exited the Svnagogve holding assuringly onto one another. The wedding carriage door opened by the brides oldest nx i.e brother Nellie looks into his eyes, joy all over her person turns and uses the American custom with her eyes tosses up high and outward towards the wedding attendees, the bridal bouquet.

Isidor relieves him of the door, gets in the carriage behind his new bride and glances at his brother-in-law relieving of the temporary honor of protector and off goes the twaining couple to future bliss, fortune and fame.

That moment led to a main character in chapter two. Isidor and Nelle Gohen were the birth characters of Bartholamew "Bat" Masterson.

The grant had arrived one month ago. The colonal kept it under armed guard the Smitsonian had arranged with the president to have grants skeletal remains transported by amxed guard to Massachusetts where it would be properal examined, packed and shipped to the museum.

Chief Thomas and Blique were insulted it turned out to just another reason to go war.

All the major nations were on the warpath when Colonal Graff gave Custer orders to go with the remains to Massachusetts.

While two days out a great cloud of smoke arose behind the departed troops. Custer left ten privates with the remains and headed back to the fart. Not in time not a soldier of civilian remained alive. Revenge came to mind but the entire garrison had lost to the on the path of death and destruction. If would be suicide to retaliate Custer mustered the remnant and to full gallop returned to the privates. Then traveled on east. Forty two troopers, a dead giants skeleton and oneself promoted Li-tenant Colonal George Armstrong Custer.

CHAPTER FIVE

It was told now that the Little Big horn had given the Indian Nations a blow that could not be recovered from. The United States government put on the full press. More troops and arms were sent to mop-up the tactics worked. Outnumbered from the start more and more soldiers came west to protect the new settlers. Settlers believed to all be from the eastward board, but in truth Ireland, Finland, Scotland, Germany, Itality, England, Canada were only a few countries exported people became the USA imported peoples who migrated west and enhanced the already vastly outnumbered nations. The so called redman without canons gatling guns, dynamite and other technologies had no prayer, no had not eve so much as a hope of holding onto their land. What made it course the Calvary had enlisted blacks former slaves called, Buffale soldiers and orientals from Japan, China and other eastern people called yellows by the whites. A precident was being set and followed. Follow me, blacks (enslaved) red skins (murdered and conquered) yellow (numbers limited into the territories) of those three examples only the Indians a proud people dared to retaliate in the derogatory name calling. White eyes.

That designation died with the Indians defeat a train going through the territory once owned by the six nations. With heards of bison that covered the grass laiden plains carried on old seventy year old woman. Her hair greying. Her breasts once could fill with milk for her soon to born triplets now dry shriveling and wrinkled with needed consolement from the negro train porter but instead fearing losing his good job attained a physician. With waterfilled grey blurring eyes she relayed a tale.

It started off. You see the bareness pointing with a frilly cotton gloved finger outside the train car window.

He looked to the view. Portrubed with confusion. The grass stalks were two feet high and were so as far as the eyes could as far away as the mountains fifty miles southward. Her eyes went blank but only mentally as her brain recanted the present and allowed visions of only the past.

That'll keep them from feeding each others said a young red head beauty. The beauty could have reached the saged age three and a half years.

No disagreement was voiced. No disagreement was made no rumination. What largely devastated pity for the lands inhabitants was the pride of illuminating the obstacle called the red skinned savages.

The low motive had traveled from Washington DC and now its engines were silent. The train itself rested on its steel track. On the top of train cars were two hundred rifle armed sharp shouters. Surrounding the train on both sides, in front of the engine and behind the caboose were over four hundred thousand bisons, adults bulls male and cows and their calves. Hundreds were lying flat on the prairie grassland and hundreds more would soon be. For they were the contracts the rifleman were fulfilling. Slaughter every one of them, said the Senators, Congressman, The House of Representatives and elite business man.

The train sat still as long as live bison crossed at the railways path.

The commission on railway travel planned the route the trains were to travel on. Their reasoning was then taking place. More trains are on there way to eliminate the other heards crossing. The men were hired until there were so few the savages could not eat, could not clothing of the heards and the wooly hinds could not warm them in the deadly snowy seasons.

The auburn haired, bustled, bonnet wearing grey eyed twenty two year old, six months expecting young newly wed a year ago bride only knew with all the shouting going outside stop train, her young rifleman had taken a hundred cartridges and he had better not fall of the top so as to return to her comforting self.

The attack of their settlement settled in. There she was, four month old Joseph Josiah sleeping in his rockable bed made by her father Josiah Amos and her house was the first to receive a couple of lit projectiles. Quick as that happened others were shouting injuns, injuns, guttersal grunts happened. Men and women were being attacked. As told to do by the men giving the lectures on what to do in case of Indian attack, she headed for the rifle, but chose to leave it be. She had seen the fire arrow stuck into the wall beside the front window.

Shaking herself to get it together she threw a kiss to her baby, mouth to hand, hand wave to him and out the front door she went with rope handle of the bucket in her hand for water. The water bucket quenched, she returns to the house douses the flame. In the window she sees a brave reaching for her child, running into the house the Indian sees her as his head jerks, a caliber forty fiver from her husband, pistol douses the braves life. She guess for the child. No! he yells points to the rifle. As she hesitated a hunting knife rips the threat of the baby's father. Surprise on his dying face. Horror indurates the recent window. Calmness, somehow glows on the susceptible cheriblike infant, still in slumber.

The telegraph arrives Ob, the twelve year old sherriff's son is employed to deliver the message. He dashes to her. He does not read only delivers. She gives him ginger cookie and he awards he with a yellowing smile. He boy is working in the general store and see Oh pass. He is not is an area where he can see his mother lying on the floor lying on her side and partially on the floor is the telegram.

It is short. Gladys, your mother and father were killed in street robbery. Send your wishes. Orin Wrestley, Pastor Mount Belinda Breth Chapel.

Her legs are wide open. Her woman's private part is a bald spot. Above the bald spot is a thick, dark, silky forest of hair. His face draws closer to the opening. His fingers approach with the adroitness and accuracy of a professional. She jerks screams, screams and screams again. It is ten fingered, ten toes, two eyes, and two years bouncing baby boy. He grandson is delivered.

Beside his steady income. He had done something most people had not even heard of. He sent money to his mother's home city for investment. Sure it was a risk and it chilled his body's soul and sprit thinking he may lose it on a bad investment or that the company he had invest his money would go bankrupt. Chase invested his money in a business in Texas, Lukey Oil Refinery.

His investment paid off and he received a minimum of fifty dollars every month for the last sixty years. He was feeling elated. He was man of his domain, taking care of his wife, his four young ones and his mother.

It is Saturday. It is two days before his mothers fortieth birthday. He and Lorraine his wife with Emma Louise, Solylia Barbara and Hennie his youngest went to the bank to withdraw money so each of the could pick a gift for their grandparent. He, Lorraine and Jedadiah the oldest who was keeping grandma busy while the gifts were being gotten would sign a happy birthday together. Maclennon a well known robber had been denied entry into the Jessie and Frank James gand due to his cager exceptance of killing people while robbing them.

No one knew his features who was not close to him. His two partners collected over forty six thousand dollars as he held the two six shooters are persuasion.

The teller opened the safe, so none of the explosive were won't. He sneezed as his men where about to leave. He Pee Shorter a code name and took away the bundled dynamite. He pulled out fuses the fear of his actions caught the people insides the attention including. The husband, wife and their three getting upset about no money for grandma's gifts.

He placed the dynamite on the floor just inside the bank door. Held the door open with the bank guards chair.

Turning to ride off to catch up to his cohorts his bullet rang precise. None inside the bank survived.

When the funerals took place the lawyers concluded the paperwork and gave them to heat the graves site of her son, daughter-in-law and three grand daughter. Jedadiah would be owner of the oil stocks therefore the monthly dividends. Those would make him in the top ten richest boys in the wild west. She has guardianship over him and the monthly dividends. The general store became Jedadiah's before the funeral. She was guardian over that too.

The only consolation to her was he grandson's financial future was absolutely secure. She sat on her porch her hair had turned all but totally grey when the postman gave her the mail.

Seeing it was from her view you would think an old woman was carried out. Not her. She drencher Miss Macfarland's dress's shoulder. He was killed by bandits in an ambush in Texas.

His country was in danger there so he joined the Texas Ranger's.

Bartholomew "Butch" Cavendish and or a or more than one member of the Cavendish Gang had murdered her last relative.

The old woman's mind returned, finally freed from her past. The tall grass was still being chugged by the locomotive. She said to the doctor. He seeing her mind now at ease. The grass is there, but there is nothing but barrenness. Her had with deliberateness and with languidness placed both of her hands flat on dress between her closed legs. At that her eyes never left those of the old unringed finger physician.

CHAPTER SIX

He flushed the toilet, I will not allow a lock inside and show you what the swirling downpour of freshwater inside the commode excommunicated hope that makes you feel a little bit better, a bit more at ease with my story here. Not the same type of ease he felt when his constipated bowels finally pushed hard enough to force his tightness into enough of a circular expansion for him to finally reach his hand at grip the crapping paper.

His type of ease came accompanied with pain of an unevenly torn anus pore. As was evident at hard. Meaning bright red droplets coloring parts of the toilet paper which were moreso than the slight yellow feces. He mused to his lonesome, at teast I ain't leaning over nor to wipe at you can you believe, a grown man not only talking of but to his butt? Somewhere on this great big planet is a amusing anecdote there.

Finally at ease enough stand to his feet.

The young man let out a low sounding whom. He muttered that one hurt. Once his belt was secure he holsted his gun. It had been in his hand since he entered the indoor facility. It was in his hand a short time back when his straining tortured him so much that he sounded a long uunnnhhh and tilted sideways while still sitting and pushing. He maleness having been so insured by his past actions that the thought of a pregge came to his mind. He barely needed shrug in contemplation to neglect it except for a, how do they do it?

He emerged and with open eyes raised both his arms high up into the air. His hands high above his head, he will never forget these few words.

Henry McCarty, I have this warrant for immediate arrest, all the ten men had short barreled shot guns pointed at him. Pointed directly at him. Less than six feet and yet they all felt ill at ease.

CHAPTER SEVEN

Time came when Maximillion Perez Feliz Gonzales Estreo, decided Mexico must avenge the loss of to Antonio Lopez de Santa Anna, that led to Mexico's fall and being taken from the people of Mexico to be a part of Loss Estados de Unidos.

First move buy the government's secret service in order to assinate President Abraham Lincoln.

Make slavery a part of the agenda strengthening the being reborn south. Declare alliance with the Democrats by not allowing slavery in the reconstruction of Mexico, keeping the Confederate states of America strong.

Partnership in oil and cattle to secure the Democratic confedacy's southern border with a seasoned army and trained young guocho's to secure the New Mexican Land. His plan was working. Every country was shocked at Lincoln's assassination. His one mistake was the Secret Service was controlled by Republican's who thought Lincoln an idiot to be used to keep their more prominent people from being targeted for murder during the Civil war.

That plan solidified after the war, some speculated the Confederates might try to regain control upon Lincoln's death letting the reason and or excuse for the war to re-exist. Thus before the agreement to remove Lincoln from the presidency many safeguards were installed in business and in government in the USA and citizens of the USA supplanted in foreign countries the Mexican Estreo's plan failed when one night while tucking their two children eleven and four years old, there house and they were destroyed by a gas explosion that laid a six bedroom three story high large hacienda to sand sized rubble, Lincoln had only minute before assassinated. Apparently one of the fail safes was initiated successfully Melman J. Brown had played an instrumental part in the preparation of the assassination. He was to go back Bovie, Maryland where he owned almost half the large manufacturing of shoes hats and clothing businesses. He was given the the orders to keep his employers from consorting in what may have been motousness he took with Adel, his unattractive looking helpmate of thirty years from the mansion in Arizona and did his job well.

Robert Blake, a skilled killer with knives explosives and poisons was introduced to him in Arizona a month before his return to Maryland. It was straight forwardly told to him Blake's place in this world.

The day the Brown's departed their private car on the train, who did Melman see standing or the platform in eastern regalia buying a newspaper, but Blake.

Telman Brown was no fool. He did his part and he was excellent in doing so.

Hamilton Jelican, had an idea. It was implement but received no official title. The public during the seeding never knew of the existence. Seven hundred deceptive men and women were paid well and trained in espionage even better. They were placed as missionaries, reporter's for American News agencies, mid-range businessman, gamblers and a good number as harlots paid-to-pay. They were glamorous expensive and effective. There will be a much larger number of them in the future. They are now and in the future as long as this country stands as a native are a must.

Names were kicked to call the secret organization. It was decided no name would be given only a code sign so rare it could easily be recognized by each other though very few knew any of the others. One title Jelican held dear but negated it too was a central Intelligence Agency.

Commander Admiral Herrecic Wexler owned to large cargo ships, large enough to transport people and cargo from one continent in the western hemisphere to the eastern hemisphere. Had owned ten but the war caused the confederate government to seize eight. All ten would have been legally seized to support the confederate war efforts but two were in Japan and Wexler ordered them held from American waters.

The eight now confederate controlled shipped had been converted into battleships.

On three different battles all were sunk by land cannon or union naval fleet ships.

Wexler was recruited by the first Director of the Secret Service. After the death of Lincoln, he became a very prominent cog in the spy services for overseas secrecy. No longer did he have to gather information for the US governments secret service to fight the use of confederate currency and solidify the US republic dollar.

CHAPTER EIGHT

While passing through New Orleans Sallie Ride a pioneer newspaper woman made acquaintance with Lumulle Oscar Pulitzer, the one and only famous Arizona kidd. His gun hands had met no match. His wit was quick, keen and easy to rile. A year as a artilleryman in the army taught him it is better to kill a man close up even when behind him.

Ride interviewed the kid for the Boston observer out of Massachusetts.

A few pleasantries and then the real question she wanted answered. Her own curiousity was the only reason and her mind being picked, picked the right spot. Lom. She was about to ask again ma'am. Please address me as Arizona. I like the feeling it carries. I apologize Sallie said, measuring his sincerity. Arizona how do you like it having that anonym Arizona, while living here in New Orleans, a short space in time a short pause and she finished the question, Louisiana?

I gonnard a bank robber. He and some other were in the towns bank cleaning it out. I saw it from across the street. When they ray out the one with the most of the banks bags I shot him with a rifle I took off one of the getaway horses. His head looked kinda funny when the shell went through it. One pointed his pistol at me. Seeing me, the size I was changed his mind. He reigned up turned and went to follow the other two of his partners. I shot him in the back of his head. I was seven years old then.

Guns just took to me. Fist too. Later I fourteen and Jethro Clampett grabbed my girls breast at the dance. People saw it. So I did I. When she ran out, the people were admonishing him. His father took a strap to him.

He must have thought that was all. I went to his daddy's rarch and waited to be alone with him. We got to fisting it, he died from it.

I could not tell people it wasn't me my hands were real swollen and sore too boot. Dad made me leave. Gave me a fast sturdy pony. Eighty dollars and his colt side arm. I got to be famous in cards and guns. I did hear or occasions of a kid called Colt. One called Rawhide and another who toated the monicker Two Guns. Later I found all four of us use two side guns. All of were damned near superhuman at speed and never missing.

I do not fear the day we go up against each other. I do not relish it either. So after six years word come to me my momma had died and been put in the ground I went back. Some expressed my fame. Some tried me. Then did not but once or twice most wanted me to adhere to their new way of all for one and one for all. What I saw of their togetherness you might say, I straight laced detested it was socially clear I did not fit. I looked into my mother demise. My dad his heart just plumb broke. I buried and left. When I was on the trial I caught the train in Pulsar and saw in the newspaper my picture. There I was standing being glorified with a new moniker. Arizona kidd returns to the west. It suck.

Before I landed in Arizona, I got sickened with grief and hatred. There I stood eye shot Missouri with a name gone on ahead of me. A name of a place I ain't even welcome. I am still traveling. Headed to Paris, France. Got hired to co-star on stage next to the likes of Myra Maybelle Shirley Reed Starr, Phoebe Ann Moses and Martha Jane Canary. Heck woman. The pay is enormous.

Went through Mabelline once. Took a tour. I had the spare time. On the tour was the diggings of Miss Moses when I just mentioned. There is was bigger than say and night Alabaster pillars held up the front porch, fifteen pillars. Twenty of the regular size home here in New Orleans could fit inside of it, it was well kept. Servants, brass door knocker a foot high. Had to weight thirty pounds. In laid in that brass were real emerald, Annie Oakley. World told by the tour guide she has owned that place for three years and in those three years have been inside her own home for nine days. The rest of the time she spends doing theatre, traveling. As I will soon be. Also I want my hedges like those I saw. A full mile in every direction surrounding the home in a maze and well trimmed. Like that bet I'll hard a dilly of a time eathching one of my misbehaving young ones.

Sallie concluded her interview sorry she had no more time. Her departure time was nearing. She handed Lumuelle a piece of cardboard paper, lavender in color and smell. Her newspapers name and address. Under that was hers with the title Lead Reporter. The Kidd handed her a white pearl handled filigreed two shot darrenger from his boot top. They heard of each other since that day but never again sat and palavered face to face. Sallie Ride when on the subject would most often say the two of the two of us have not jawed since.

CHAPTER NINE

The scream lasted a second in time. That was the total time it took to end what was to be one day a woman's death. Shotgunned down in her prime. That was the total of time it took to stop the murder and rape of a grandmother. That was the total time it took to have no need for a citizen mob's lynching. That was the total time it took to halt the burning to death of preacher and his wife and two young daughter's, that was all the time it took for the newspaper not to print the stories and picture that caused the ambush death of ten townspeople in the posse. That was the total time it took to stop a dark evenings back shooting and robbery of a card gambler and his winnings. That was the total time it took to prevent those atrocities and numerous more.

That was the total time it took to spook eleven hundred cattle on the way to be sold for slaughter. That was the total time it took for the thunderous roar accompanying that lightning flash that caused the whole of the cattle heard being driven to sale for slaughter to stampede.

The shout frantically called to those who could hear. Stamped!

Scurrying to saddles to mount horses was the norm for that emergency. The thudder of the cattles running hooves and the vibrations the hooves frantic running awakened the other cowhands.

Lightning striking again and again. The partnering thunder broke out again and again. The initial loudness and bright flash is what caused the commufion. The extra striking and rearing added nothing to the mostly ordered charge of the animals. Thousands charged off with freight, but they ran together orderly in one direction. Mostly, that unidirectional charge aided the cowpokes in the putting them back in a still and calmed heard of future food and shoes and jackets and such. Bob Mendelson sat on saddle setting Hnery Gibbons left broken leg. The stampede only semi caused the break. He broke it after all had settled get off his horee.

Some of the cocks pets and pans were being retrieved. Salt was of no use spread over the prairie dissolved from the rain.

Marn Mothlee, the trial boss was surveying what needed to be done to restore what could be. He had given four others

CHAPTER TEN

This story is all true and I can verify it, said the great grandfather to his great grand-daughter. The was fast, fast, fast, fast gunslinger. Never ever missed what and never ever missed who he shot at. And he shot a lot of men.

He started as private in the Union army during the civil war. Mind you. He wasn't a gunslinger then.

He had been in three real big battles. Saw many men die on both sides. His side was usually the winning side. That bunch of guys he mostly fought beside got a real reputation. The blue coats, his side and the grey coats the opposite site all heard how good his boys were in battle. You can see why the greys began to hate his group. They layed out a trap for emgrandaad cane a reminding coaxing. They layed out a trap for them. He corrected.

Now those grey coats knew them blue coats were battle tried and tested, so no obvious trap would work.

The trap was the usual kind of trap, but a twist was added to it.

They greys attacked them with a few of their own soldiers a hit and run. By running the greys figured them boys in blue would chase them. As they should. So when they chased the few more would be hiding in the heavy tree cover in ambush. Here's where you got to remember them boys in blue had been tried and tested before, so they knew a trap when they one was set to close in on them. They chased the greys to the trees, but they do not inside, figuring it was a setup. They sent for two cannon to straif the trees for hidden ambushers. The cannon balls into the trees.

Now here again you need to remember those greys know the blues were not dummies and would smell that.

When the cannon came a very large number of greys ten times as many as the blues attacked those blues and the cannons, but not from the trees. They trapped them by attacking from behind the blue coats. From the direction they had come from, which was real trap anyway.

The blues, they fought hard. Fired off all their rounds the rifles held and pulled out their revolvers because that was all they had that had bullets. Only the one officers a second lievce had a sabre, sa he was slicing and stabbing as many grey coats as possible. When they got too many attacking at once for him to defend himself with his sword he went to unlatch his revolver. He was to slow and got shot four times.

Them blues lost the fight, and the cannons and what cannon balls and powder was left.

Now I told you that part to tell you the rest of the story. The real good part.

When he had started this sage she was supposed to be on her way to bed but since he was only going to be visiting for two days her parents secumbed to her pleas for great grandfather, the historical Indian fighter to regale her with a story. Yes she used the wood regale. She had learned it from Miss Susan Spencer, the school marm.

That was the only one of them blue coats lived. He healed up some. Come to clear thinking so he out some of the leather from his holster top. Started using saddle soap on the inside and the outside. Made it more supple and easier to get to the handgun. Practiced his draw everyday when he wasn't tending his bosses circle ranch. Practiced every night two, three hours. Got fast faster than a lot. Faster all of the ones he had to thrown down on. Sixteen in all. Got so good when a young gun wanted to raise a reputation on him, he started saving their lives by outdrawing them so fast, and he just shot their gun handle right before their hand could touch it. Then that he thought was worth anything. Some he knew by the way they carried their public behavior, when they went to throw down on him, he'd would shoot off the thumb of their shooting hand. Those that weren't worth a nickle who had on two guns, well he shot off the thumbs on both their hands. Word got around. Some got scared of him. Every great one gets a name to be called by ain't his own. His was Two Gun.

Lived to pass the thirtieth birthday. Most with a reputation don't.

The day come Quick Draw Pecos Larry round about twenty years old sent a message to his hotel room. More only said, middle of the street two PM. Two PM came and there was Pecos in the middle of Maine Street. Cast a shadow in front of him sixteen feet long.

Two Gun sent little Sarah Jessica a May rand out to him with a note. Note had the words. If you really must do this I will be out of the Tonsorialist in a minute.

If you're gone, then well and good, everything is just fine. If you're still in the middle of the street, well then I will shorten your shadow.

One minute past the time Sarah gave him the note out of barber's shot he came. Peco's was still in the middle of Maine Street. Son to his back.

Standing the barber shop Walkway roof over his head he Quick Draw.

Quick Draw widened his stand and readed his gun hand.

Can you see me clear Pecos he yelled. I see you right clear enough. Now lets get it on.

Blam, blam. Two shots rang out. Never heard them echo empty as the street was.

Two gun let one boot onto Maine Street. Then his other. Before he walked right up to Pecos. Pecos jerked. Most of jerked twice, there were two shots, but the shots rang so lose together you might of though there was only one.

Pecos slumped to his left. His sixteen foot shadow went to thirteen feet. Pecos slumped more. His shadow went too nine feet. Pecos's knees hit the dirt. His shadow went to four feet.

When Two Gun stood over him his shadow was directly under his but.

Well truth be fully told maybe it was near an inch and a half. That's it now. Time for bed. Signal from Grandson gotten.

Little girls are so wonderful. Mohenni sat in that wicker seated chair with her right leg, thigh and calf. Her right foot's instep cocked behind her left ankle. Her knee up wards right little hand on her knee. Left little hand on her right hand chin on her left hand. Those almost shell colored eyeballs floated in their blue seas. Good healthy upbringing.

Hugs for all the adults and a long smooch on her great grandpa chin.

What happened to that Two Guy? She asked. A quick look to the parents. An apparent approval. He became famous. Books were wrote about him. He went to Germany to protect his truths. They paid him two hundred seventy two thousand dollars for the rights to publish and sell those books. He now travels to most of the important literate countries for dinner's in his honor. Soon as he can he visits his family to make sure every ones in good stead.

Her dad peeps her peeping him peeping her presses his hands together reminding her to give the Hombre upstairs his due.

Water these days come out of a hard house in the bathroom in square to wash. He did shower. Thinking of Mehenni he rubs his fingers over four small dots a little indented.

He remembered his grand daughter and his grandson-in-law.

Smiling he remember the sign the grandson-in-law gave to his great grand child and mimicked.

CHAPTER ELEVEN

The army escort had delivered their cargo. Very few were appraised of the giant man's fifteen foor remains. Lopitious Pediman, the museum curratod had cautioned the Lieutenant Colonal. Secretarial of the United States or the Colonal who sent custer with the ones had died in the attack on the fort. All the other calveryman with Custer transporting the remains east were not with Custer when the remains were taken from the Indian's land and brought to the fort. Only Custer had the true knowledge of the amazing cargo. He was under orders never to divulge the existence of the deal man's remains. The US government big wigs promoted him and sent him to areas out west. The most dangerous places in the country. Most men sent there would not live more than two years. The last push to excise the territory had just began.

General George Armstrong Custer's silence would become assured at Pinhead Creek, splitting Waters, Little Bigttorn or Sweet Water. He would pose no threat to hiding the existence of giants having once walked the Earth. Custer's was never to learn of the acquisition of the other giants human remains over the past six decades. All had been classified Top secret. The former presidents, the sitting president and hopefully no future president were told nor would be told. The temporary office he held or would be elected to hold need not know due to mankinds uneasy demeanor to the strangers. No president would he trusted with what this security free was striving to uncovered. But, who were these men and women and what was the name of their organization. In the Cemetary lye secrets. Secrets only those invited may call on. This is one of those rights. Secret service Agent Sethma Blye has drawn the assignment to wear the Persian stone. The ball at the Hotel Rint is for multidegreed college professionals. This meeting is in ascertain of the guess in furtherance which are in position for an open sodalities to their secret society. A special type is searched-east about. The recognition and depth of knowledge pertaining to this particular carcanet.

Big tops Lorettz young would not have been thought of to make the grade. Big tops was the escert. The extremely high paid social climber. She was in attendance latched to the left bicep of Stanton O. O'Malley, thee premiere movie director.

O'Malley has been genious approved for his entire adult life and most of the adolescent one was in the company of notable businessman. The lesson he was most adroit at verifying his knowledge is attached to his arm.

His entire professional career on his arm one of if not thee most expensive and highly well known courtesan. No sexual harassment slanders for him. Business wise his reputation never was tarnished with a non disclosure agree and no lawsuits. His name is the business community stolid.

Misjudgement of a person's statis is an absolute bitch. Big tops took notice of the necklace. She guided her date close enough to a small gathering of champagne flute holders. Her eyes lit up and sethma always sharp caught the glint in the emerald greens.

In the minor elite financial circles the courtesian was widely known and a well established fixture at the higher class social gatherings. To most of her few, a hundred or a little less friends she at a time eight or so years back she was on the fast track from porn queen to that of thee pornography goddess. To her college schools she had graduated cumlaude for her associates in communications. Cumlaude for her bachelor degree at New York University. Magna cum laude for her masters in history at Stanford. Summa cum laude at New York University in ancient history placing second in her graduation class.

One might inquiries of how she got the name Big Topps, her natural physical fifty double c-cups proved she earned that as a matter of factly allonym. The thing only her sugar Daddy's could tell you is those tops were spongey, soft and they stayed, poking outward without consistant bralessness there was no degree of difference. Perfect in symmetry, perpendicular to her ribcage and parallel to the white arc rose marble bar counter top where young and Blye now conversed on men, money and world monopolizing. Blye admitted she had not expected young to be so well acquainted with her necklaces history. One would hardly notice it. It has almost no attractive physical attractiveness. Yes but it is worth an untold fortune and no one has seen it almost two thousand years.

My opinion is not to ask where and how I obtained it, said Blye. But of course was big topps Young's reply.

Blye saw her date musing of the two of them. You date said Blye. Blye gave Young an address. You can meet there if you really want to know. Then dislodged her temptation than mingled with the other invites.

One really qualified candidate. Of all the investigated, three stood out two other females and an Idian refugee who was a guest of Senator Ben Oglethorpe and Mrs. Mei Oglethore a fifty one year old Japanese girl no one san, of the Japanese Emperor, in her first month of seven month trip. She was the better of the four choices. The reason she could not be selected this top secret organization would not admit a non-American. Big Topps Loretta Young.

Four scientist were to go out west to visit the digging site of Project Flea, this was the code given the fifteen foot giants skeleton.

None were told the trip was only planned but it was a farce to dupe the new inductee into a slot of security test. They were simple and they were thorough. The Indian uprising had been known were going to happen for over a year. The US government gave the red savages no way out of war thus no way out of obitertion. That excuse cancelled the four's trip out west.

What really shut down all the excuses the four came up with to go anyway. We are not cowards. Knowledge sometimes force scientist and explorers to take chances. Then the news came Yellow hair, the monicker tagger to General George Armstrong Custer, had been killed at the massacre of the little Big Horn. The great Indian fighter and their would be protector could no longer protect anyone.

The four never did past their traveling expedition gear and on the eve of getting the news of Custer's demise young was having dinner with an old friend of her families son. His name was John Wasley Crockett, whose father her families old friend had met a similar demise at George A Custer.

His father David who historically never enjoyed being called Davey, did in the US war against Mexico in the Alamo battle.

At this moment was all the message read that was given to young upon she and young Crockett, that was deciphered. Everything is a go.

That bones were already safely stored in a vault. As enormous vault full of historical artifacts the general public was never to acquire their knowledge.

The member of the societies top secret existence who had to be replaced had died of goute in Samalia, Africa.

Their New Zealand spring lamb watered their appetites. The dinner eaten. The wines consumed. The night together was nothing other than a savory memory, as they departed each others company forever.

CHAPTER TWELVE

Colt Meyers once the fastest gunslinger in the. Many men made their mark in history with either or both the rifle or the handgun. Their were nutches on all of them. They never faced each other in a one on one quickdraw to the death. If there were only a worldwide talent fastdraw and anyone with the reputation of killer must attend Colt Meyers would walk away prize winner. Not Ringo, who might be the last of the gun play Paladins would be so great in history.

But on this day a sun up Colt Meyers could not answer that would be call. Colt Meyers lies face down in the dust in a suburb of Houston, Texas. The back of his heads hole an inch and a half opening shower a once cream colored now ruby red shredded piece of muscle.

The ambush was a total surprise to the rest of the world. He had just paid Melonie "Bliss Lips" chang double the price of an evenings activities.

Meyers when going to her asked how much for the whole nights festivities, while eyeing her middle was a smile thirty dollars agreed. Lets go.

Chang was one exceptionally beautiful four feet nine inch Philipean. Nineteen years old. Two years in America. Eleven years in the business of the body's sexual arts.

In her room she was a molded beauty naked, clean, slim, small nipples and the scent of oils that only disgusised cleanliness.

Only one thing did she with hold, her backside. No! no! no do in tombong. No in tumbong. He said, what the hell is no? no in butt. Me no in butt no tumbing her finger pointing to in, the other hand held up palm towards her patrons face while vigorously shaking her little sexy face left to right. Making certain her objections being understood. Colt Meyer's got the message. He looked. Her posterior was really flat. No sign of ever being entered into.

A couple of hard worked hours had gone by before he did it, he grabbed bliss hipps, pinned her face down on a chain, held her arms behind her back with one what must have been giant sized hand in her mind and forced his rod into her back trailroad. He rammed her and rammed her over and over holding her mouth in the seat of the chair until no more screaming for him, no tumbling. She could not scream more just cry. When he decided he pulled his road out. There on the tip od his penis was evidence any court would except that he had her rear end opening around his manhood. He yanked face from the chair. Her eyes closed, tears rolling down her face and still sort of gasping at the treatment. Her pulled head backwards to the back of the chair and as he lifted her to place her bottom on the chair seat that evidence on the top of his penis disappeared along the part of meatrod. Hidden by her lips and behind her parted teeth. She swallowed without knowing what was soon to make acquaintance with her earlier dissolving Asian culsine.

He was not done yet. The night's stars still lingered. He repeatedly went on with the business she was in and the deal the two had made.

Light came up. He had her kiss is trousers wear his well taken care of piece was now comfortably covered and walked carelessly out of her room, down the stairway across the entrance floor and cut the door. A few seconds later a loud thunderlike gun powder blast roared.

Melonie Chang saw no one about the street so she carried her rifle back to her bedroom. She placed in under her bed where she usually stored, washer her mouth out and went back to bed. Usually when she turned in after a night's business, she would drift off to sleep thinking just another night on the western frontier. As she did this early morning only the thought she had sarcasticly. Only this day break she was hurting of a torn rectum, crying from being brutalized and sore or heart.

CHAPTER THIRTEEN

Dust streamed through the old west, stamped cattle, blew away from their pogs many wigwams and in few choking clouds of dust some men and fewer women were actually made blind by sand, pepples, dirt and other objects forced into the eyes of those unprepared for such ruckus blown and flown by the hundred an hour or more winds.

A rumor had come about in one unknown towns newspaper that those deadly windblown objects led to the idea of wearing a mask for protection. Not the ones were your eyes and nose opening were facilitated to block those small objects from causing permanent nerve damage but rather to hide the face or faces of highway man, train and bank robbers.

No reports were written to my awareness that any records exist on the subject of how delighted those of the early, mid and late eighteen hundreds lauded the wind and dust streams. Perhaps they did not think the way you and I do in today's enlightenment. I would agree though you might argue that only I have such thoughts.

Putting it together you should think that tens of thousands of cowboys and let us recall the efforts and effects of cowgirls applaud those dust and Windstream days and nights.

List a couples good reasons and they had to have categorized, no cattle stealing dust wind and dust storms, no bank robbings and the banks would have been closed with the townspeople hold up inside their homes did you get the "hold-up" no showdowns and no raping their wives and daughters while you were out on the ranch or for any other reason the man would have been out of the house. Maybe some of the lesser bedroom satisfied wives may not agree with the last one. Yes. I wrote maybe. How would I know for one hundred percent. I was not born until nineteen fifty three. Uh, too close to home? Do not blame me I give you this one way out. We are reading and writing a proposal the cowboy story only. I bet where he should have felt fire breathing down his back that he felt some relief

CHAPTER FOURTEEN

Hot, hot. Blazing hot in town today. Minton forrest said Amuel Just. Howdy Minton, just let ho. You in town to put your bid in for Mayor? Sure seems to me like a good position have, but no. leave to Mann and Frederricks to fight it out on there own. I'll abide to who wins. Just let out, you'd be the better man. Better than the two of thems good ideas on their best days. Thanks just. Remembering the mans name he halted his words and held back. Just the same, I'll stay out of it. I'll stay out of it is all he said on the election.

That one for one the school ma,'s students? Promised I'd do one for each of um. Guess I'll mosey on over to the bar for a cold beer. Forrest was walking off. Town needs you forrest. Amuel Just called to him as he walked on.

Just leaned back on his chair and continued to white as he was when Minton Forrest had walked up to him.

Amos White was on the other side of the street about to go into Chinese laundry. It came him. The light in his brain made him take notice. So he naturally questioned. He forced a few thoughts that came to him out of his thoughts he wanted to be real sure. That is right he concluded as he stopped at the laundry's front entrance way. Amuel is not wearing his six shooter since a little bit after Miss Jennie came to town to teach school. Amuel Just was the retired town marshall was slick and lightning quick. Even when he quit the job he toted his colt eleven ninety nine for years. A smile came to his lips and he went on in.

Vote for Abraham Frederricks poster was on the north wall to his left.

One more step inside and on the south wall to his right side was the poster of Mattlock Mann. Mann for Mayor.

Good day to you Ames White. How ale you today (caution reading this part please. It may appers as Asian racism. Please put understanding that in that early peved many Asians who had recently migrated to the west had not mastered the pronunciation of the western English. This is my attempt at holding the periods authenticity. I pray you do not judge me for my attempt as the possibility you can believe and or even insist on the wrong view. Thank you)

Fine to middlin Mister Zheu, his name on his cleaners plackard and on the wall behind his counter was Nian Zheu. The name and type if business in the Chisnoiserie style.

The two men briefly hold neighborly talk. Their differences could still be visualized even by the blind man. White's voice was high and throaty. White's tall man visage six feet five and a half, Zhau five feet six inches and of foreign ascent. There were in different order. White referring to the cleaner's work you do excellent Zhau. Zhau way. Yes work is excellent that I perform.

Walking out the door white again took note of the politician voting posters Abraham's Fredderick's on his right side now rather than his left as it was when he entered. Mattlock Mann's now on his left. Politicians, his sarcastic remark at how some flip flop once they have gotten elected. His trust of them went that far and no further.

Perhaps the interest that Nian Zhaw disclosed on that very same day was the synergy allowing American Asians finally the right to vote in such an election.

While in the laundry as on a number of other occasions white saw the door on Zhau's left hand side but behind the business counter.

The same today as every other day when white and every other person who entered Zhau's laundry the little bell above the doors inside and above the door yet low enough for the entranceway door to come into contact with the lower wider part of the bell pushing it forward. The thin chain attached to the top smaller area of the bell held the bell from falling, allowed the bell's forward motion causing the clapper inside the bell to hit one of areas clapper inside the bell to hit one of areas rather than simply hand downward. The clapper caused the bell to ting alerting the propriorter someone has entered into his establishment. The chain also allowed the bell to return to its inert hanging position but not before it tinged the bells opposite side giving the le. The completion to the bells tingle completing the alert to the proprietor. The same process of sounds again happened when the door closed.

Behind that door to Zhau's left was Ming da Zhao, Nian's wife and though at that time was not given officially the status but also his partner in business and Rhue En Li his older daughter of nine years and Phu Shi Hahn, his younger son

On the wall behind that also antiqued white jade hooks faded by time on a full two feet above Pho's upward reaching hands was a brand spanking new gun. The shells full of glass, small sharpened jagged pieces of brass and dehydrated cyanide.

There was this type of day in the old west when no camels' attitudinal behavior was in need of an imported driver. When no indigenous medicine men were weaving the final straws to war. When no innocent men or women were lynched for a crime one did not. When no fast gun showdowns left men dead in the dirt street. When no trains or banks were robber. When no cattle were rustled. When the rod man was not systematically place in the cup of genocide. When the weather did not sting. When the likes of Custer her not honorably killed in battle and the battle called a massacre. When crabs and stench did not take over a man's pride. When whores in the ill repote distrist did not exist. Yes there were those days, but the days when those undertakings took place is not what this script has been about.

I hope I have in some way somewhat entertained you.

I do with pleasure thank you for your patronage and your valuable time.

Sincerely
Rodney Paul Williams

This book's author

PREVERT – PART 2

CHAPTER ONE

In the inner workings of this planet Earth something major has gone away.

God found that out the hard way.

People believed those that did believe thought that God was perfect. That he could not make a mistake, but that has been proven incorrect.

You can ask why me a full Christian, one who totally believes in God's existence could bring himself to put such a thing, a byte of infortion as the above in print.

Take as gospel, I did, and I am not the first one which explains without a doubt that I am not the only one.

Should I even again as prior to this time and together inclusive with this time write on God I write what I can prove to be so.

Where do I hide such proof? It is not a hidden fact but in the everyday plain sight of the Holy Bible, and what is written within its covers.

If anyone and I write including God does something on purpose and then verbally admits to all the masses after he has done it complains that it grieved him, than I must say even I myself had done something and wish I had not, a mistake was made.

God created man and woman. It was done on one of the six days of creation before he took a rest on the seventh, Sabbath, day.

God found that man was... so, he made it rain forty days and forty nights.

Please God in all the sins done by myself and my direct blood line, please forgive us? Thank you.

The thank you art, I was thought by the woman you loaned to me to bring me to you. She did. Thank you from us all!!

CHAPTER TWO

You see that sixty eight year old very, very handsome old guy sitting on those steps on the Vandelorian Majestic Suites building there. He is a great man. So you may come up with adversity to me describing him as being great. Solely because there are some fifty heavy duties trash bags sitting on the rear paved way to the suites.

He is there by his choice. His own volition. He had been there for all of twelve minutes awaiting the RINO is a private company contracted to the whole of the cities most influential business and skyscraper rentals.

RINO is Mafia owned and operated. It is part of the mob's dual decoded protection rocket.

No better place for his reasoning for waiting on the spot. The kenetics of his brain allotted this area to be perfect. His thoughts and his thoughts only.

There were no cameras in this alleyway. He did not drink. Nor did he smoke. His hands had on each two rubber surgery gloves. No possible way to alert any of his being there, no DNA would be left when he left.

His class would allow him no eating and or drinking here. His cleanliness of personality kept him from urinating, even in a bottle he could cap, nor a coffee cup with a lid. Defecating too was not a vehicle he had succumbed to.

His only clue that he had been there is his singing of the new national anthem for the United States, Written by Country western super superstar Toby Keith, Courtesy of the Red, White and Blue, yet non heard him as this one the one time he quieted his voice on the lyrics of his favorite rendition.

The old national anthem sucke nard. The ending of a thought had occurred as the diesel of the RINO engine came into his ears.

The truck got to the mound of refuse and he picked up a full hefty bag then tossed it into cavernous waste receplicle. He then helped put in the rest of the trosh, waved the guys and the thickly built Puerto Rican female off as the truck rambled on to its next destination.

I guess not he had thought of his musing earlier weather married women on a beach during the hotness of summer in their thong bikinis wear their wedding rings should their husbands not be present.

He felt just the slightest bit empty as he made his left turn on departure from the alley. No answer had come to him.

Partial overcast brought out the sun glasses.

His plan was so well thought he noticed what seemed to be a homeless man sitting on a double high milk crate seat with of all things a shoe shine kit, but passed up the chance. No need to push it.

On his merry way he went. Satisfied his crime will never be uncovered.

She was on the Seattle Washington Downtown Circulation bus. There were a couple of cons doing a three card Monte hustle. She did not need the money but decided to break them anyway. Send them back to wherever they came from.

She stood along side of the gamer and the cards as she had been taught. I have three hundred dollars she said. Can I play? She asked. Show the color of your money the card handler said. She brought out a one hundred dollar bill. Sat it on the makeshift corrugated board.

The card handler started shifting the three cards showing a queen and two jacks. One red and one black.

Where is your money she asked of him? He brought out a folded wad and placed two fifty's beside her Franklin. Before we go on she softly said, where I come from you guys give odds. You're supposed to be the one with fast hands, so no problem. Two too one he said. No she replied three to one.

His game was to alleviate her that cash so he boldly put up three hundred. She toughed the left card to her and won. He felt like an ass.

Give you a shot at losing the rest of your wad she said. The bait is set.

I have four hundred. You want to cover it. One of his backmen watched a little closer while at attempting to be only slightly interested. That is how she found which of the twenty or so passengers he was. She was still watchful. There may be a third.

He again brought out his was. Two too one he said. She replied no, she put three hundred of the four in her pocket. You want your money. It's going to cost you to try and get it back. One C-note at a time. Fine he said. Putting up two hundred. No way. Five to one. Then she put the full four hundred on the corrugated. I can't cover the whole two g's he said.

Ok what you can. He put up six hundred dollars. She took back two hundred. Three too one she said. Deal he said. No backing away was a three card Monte player trait and she knew.

She picked up the eight hundred dollars after she chose the red queen without a doubt.

The stir on the bus ended in a minute. She sat down in the bus's last row of seats.

She had again as since the first day of moving into a Seattle a year ago told mental note of the public transits bus's cleanliness. Not like filthydelphia she again came to the realization that people here were better than those in Pennsylvania where she was born and raised.

Sadness hit her to remember that place but the joy of her surroundings kicked that feeling to the curb. Not a clean curb like the ones where she now abided, but a trash, needle and empty drug container covered sidewalks like the ones she moved away from.

She stayed alert and rode the bus to the end of the line where the three of the Monte card crew got off.

Her inner smile glowed all over her. She stayed on and rode the same transit back to her actual stop. Since they did get back on, figuring she must have been wise that they might have robbed her to get back there lost ungains, so she released her three eighty from he hand in her jacket pocket.

She would not be the hero on this day.

Laura Bettison, the transit driver also seemed to show some relief. She had watched.

CHAPTER THREE

Her complete nakedness showing she reached for one of the smaller hot pink towels dampening her wet from the shower hair. Picks up another from next to the wicker hamper where the first one was tossed and makes hat of it. Then she dries her pubs with the wash cloth. Discards it into the same hamper. As she adjust the full body towel around he once naked and still dripping water body she again pays attention to her wrap around sound coming from the super hero movie she has on her living room projected screen the sound happens still. She knows nearly every line and yet there are sounds.

The actors voices. Talking to each other. Holding conversations not on tapes that were recorded when the movie was first filmed. The conversations do two things. They both progress from the last viewing carrying on their talks with the left off one when the projector was turned off and also new ones occur current events of the historical happenings of today.

The one thing that clouds her mind in why do the talks go on from where they had left off before. Why do they not converse with each other while the movie was turned off and she had slept or cavorted outside. One other thing began to totally worry her. On occasion they characters in the movie reminded her of her own thoughts she had had on a scene when that scene was again played as though she was being included. She began to test it, she commented to the movies characters on the comments made to her. They in turn were not discourteous. They replied.

This better be a tall drink of water or I am subject to hang up the phone. Those were the words that sub-angrily told her the phone was ringing. It was personalized ring tone. She changed her ring tone almost every day. She was one who became bored very posthaste and basically hell-for-leather and no apologia necessary.

She often used many synonyms for her quickness of being bored in conversation. The only one she purposely chose to neglect was lickity-split phrase, deciding that would never bring on her lackadaisical trait.

Hi auntie Em, call Celeesze's small mezzo soprano love call. Cel, as her aunt called her was nine years old. An appraised, tested and certified genious and a future, near future sure to an operatic superstar. Cel's favorite musical instrument though did not fit her future in musical expertise, which by the way she had mastered to perfection was the Bass guitar, which also somehow did not fit her lead voice when singing her favored country western music.

You coming? Went the musical inquisition. Mom says you are. Dad said you are, and you said you are.

Can I get a phrase or a word or two in edgewise my little love one? Cel gives silent. Naturally I'll be there, Joyousness on the other end of the phones sound waves. Can I bring something for you? Just you auntie. Love you. Dad's giving me the say help for him sign. An command he's giving me that we going to be tardy.

Some people are crazy. Or they just psychic? Going on his way to the front door Dion waves to his sister on the other end of the phone, as if she could see him making the gesture, he was socially satisfied and Celeesze's catches up to him in the door, her video game on Candy Crush.

George Blessing and extra-ordinarily attractive wife Grenda Eliz live next door to Em. George has come from the elevator heading to his door. Em gets a feeling, cracks her front door and George Blessing is passing her apartment door. She opens the door something startling him. He sees the body towel and holds his impression. Em with a beckoning forefinger halts him. He a total gentleman since they met each other eleven years ago at this very same spot, steps to her while hoping none are in her apartment demanding a violent attention.

Em, when he is a few inches from her face drops the towel, Em braces and sexually French kisses him. Deep tongued. He does pull back but it takes a few moments. One of two of those moments are due to his being surprised.

Em smile. Eyes glistening. Re-enters her apartment. The door she tries slowly to close. The towel is in the way of the door frame.

George happy, but in his state he still remembered Grenda, his Grenda and what she has waiting twenty yards and seconds away. He chose Eliz and went home.

The towel is retrieved. The door is closed. That I'll touch that hot bi---. He will fu__ you soon. He will also be thinking of me. Enjoy.

A quarter of an hour later the batteries in her vibrating double was put to rest in the pocket of the plush velvet four cushioned sofa.

The cushions were barely spotted but had a paucity of dampness. Em would never admit it, not even to herself but sometime after Grenda's husband passed her mind she had to force out the vision of three men having their way with her. Leaving her insides and cheek bones around her mandibular sore had walked away with her lying in some dank dark alleyway and robbed of her money. The part about the loss of that money she brought her out of it, those damned losers, she though with her utmost of distaste towards them. Their money was still in her jacket pocket.

She would never admit those losers caused the spotting on her, Velvet Bigouletti, sofa.

CHAPTER FOUR

The ten days and passed rapidly. A phone call every day from nurse Roberta kept the tediousness of dullness to just under overwhelming. He did the television which incorporated FM radio. He listened to the war of the worlds show done by W.K.B.W. Buffalo, New York station crew more than forty times and that closed his mind off from the dangerous situation he had landed into.

His short time taken in the first two days was totally unthought-of. He was always careful to handle such problems. The last time just before being diagnosed with the COVID- nineteen virus was no different. He handled it with precision. No witnesses. The only evidence was what he meant to leave. It would not lead to him, so he no longered himself with the aggravation that the police might easily arrest him here.

Do you have a place to go when you leave here? That question had been asked of him on three different occasions since he had checked into the hotel quarantine area. It was the sole thing that did depress him. Being asked that once was once too much. His reply to it the second time he kept to himself. I ought break your face. He forgot his reply easily enough. Shit, came from his voice box the third time. When questioned on his reply, he thought it better say nothing. He also thought it best to with the swiftness place his foot up her ass. Since it was all done by phone as not to spread virus that was not going to happen. He did not know who the people were who interviewed on his health every day.

No symptoms chose to attack him, so on the tenth day security were told that he could go home, so they escorted him on different path then the one he was escorted to his room on. Finally some real food.

It took exactly one day before he got to the understanding. Real food at this stage of COVID pandemic meant free sustenance from shelters and whatever other homeless resources there were. The riots had the grocery stores shut down. The laws closed the restaurants. If her had had family or friends he still would not have in pinged on them. They were in the same dirty as was he.

Nothing was open. He had slept in his apartment. Little food had been stored there as he had made up his mind months ago before the pandemic to forego cooking so he needed not to wash dishes. Now the restaurants that were his staple had been ordered and put out of serving by the Governor, Lousey freaking Democrat.

The last thing she wanted in her life was to go against today's societal norm, the news on the television changed her mind. The broadcasted program changing was one week earlier.

The girl been a student, at Simon Gratz, a ghetto neighborhood elementary school. The child was not in any of the classes she taught but she had seen her, noticed the child must be having home problems over those four years. She had kept her own council. Kept her mouth shut. Now the little red head was dead. Beaten to death.

The report stated the home was broken into. Invaded, robbed and the girl was the only one indoors at the time.

She had remembered her girlfriend and associate deaconess at: holy Blow founder, church telling her a guy who handled such things when the mother of an abused little one had not sufficient c__ hairs to have the authorities address the problems. Though the police were paid to handle such insufficiencies as child abuse, both physical and mental.

She sought him out. Save the child.

No answer at his door. There was a park nearby. Only three streets away. Remembering an insignificant piece of information, she pulled it together. His things he's a good father with those birds. Maybe she fed them as did most old guy gangsters in books and movies. None of the gangster molls even sat in a park distributing break crumbs and pieces of pretzels. She tried there a couple of days. No contact. On an occasion or two when there was no answer at his door, she sat in the park and by ordinance watched the people looking as bunch of bank bandits go by with their mouths and noses covered. There were some with the Seattle Supersonics logos on their face pieces. What are the words for them? Oh, yes. Masks. Masks wearing was legally mandated countrywide law. How the ones were found to fit the little children she noted none of us are truly safe. The girls wearing pink ones or lavender colored one. The boys with cowboy and super hero ones. Where are our female super hero masks she had a negative muse. Not happy in the least bit. Only enlightened. Blue on one side. White on the other side again she consorted that the little people seemed undiscomforted by those elastic bands behind the cars holding the protection stable. Unlike that of her own which pressed into the back of her ears without and appeasement to her own comfort.

Blliitt, Blliittt, Blliiitt. Hello. May I help you. He answered his cellphone. Hey guy. You alright man? Your mail is piling and some babe has been leaving you notes on your room door. Says she needs you to call her. Jethro? Yeah. Good to hear from you. I took a little when I came out of quarantine. I am in Philadelphia, Mississippi. You coming back anytime soon. I am not sure yet. Are you okay? Yeah I'm good. How's my girlfriend. Mitni is fine. She was worried a little about you. She's a great kid Jethro. Tell her I give her a shout. She'll appreciate that. What do I do about your mail and

The babes notes? Hold my mail for me, will you? You have the woman's phone number with you now? In my hand man here it is. Well wishes were given.

The two hung up their cell phones.

He kicked the unconscious villain smartly in his shattered teethed mouth with the suede steel toed, toe of his boots again that was the tenth time. Most of the teeth were now shattered his lips were the consistency of a much breakfast cereal. The four parts of his jaw bones had been shattered too. The boots had splinters of teeth and pieces of skin and flesh. They were also ruined with splotches of the victims sanguine fluid.

That job done, so before he departed two more vicious velocitied kicks with into the unconscious one's left eye. They were meant to blind that eye.

As he made his departure, the two hidden on lookers, one a six year old Asian girl, the other the child's mother. The mother is pleased. Her daughter's rapist has been the cost. The two went home from their incognito post, but first the parent stopped off at Ling's sweet Bakery and treated the little likeness and herself. Herself for getting the right man for the job. She really felt pleased with his work. The child had only talked to their hero for a couple of minutes two days ago.

Morality in this part of the world had fallen so deeply he was shocked by the reasoning he had been called in Mostly mothers of young children had no care to the rape of one or more of the offspring. They had begun to not only except the rapes but in a manner encourage them as long as an escape from their own responsibility to call the law on their child's antagonist did not land upon themselves. He looked up to that young Asian parent as his hero.

Four city blocks later in the middle of the one hundred forty block south Mitzorango way he enter the rental van.

Twenty miles away and two hours later a little boy Samuel Adams stood beside a small breasted, medium waistline super wide hipped Caucasian middle aged large rocked four carat diamond and thick wide platinum wedding ring. He gave the two a nod and two entered the econline.

Two days later the evening news reports a minor story on the break-in of the Blue county Zoo. The main gate door lock was broken and their liquor storage area was pilfered for eleven cases of alcohol.

What was never found was the extra meat the lions, tigers and leopards were fed. What was never found was the smile on his face at his musing the animals in captivity were again eating human flesh as their ancestors had done in the jungle while in the wild.

Both jobs he had been called in for were done. He was headed to the train station on his way back home to Seattle Washington.

CHAPTER FIVE

In Constitution county a suburd of Allerton Texas, Lorenzo "Lil L" Halftown almost exhausted returns to his minihacienda. Blood and both of his hands, trousers and eight thousand dollar stetso cowboy boots.

His normal routine through his adult years when returning home from a call was a sixteen ounce long neck bottle of Alabama full bodied black beer inundated will with crystals of ice. Frost on the exterior.

He would have had a couple double straight bourbons with his father a former US Marshall who died of lung cancer five years back. He was remembering those days and lied down. He fell to sleep straight away with the thought of tipping up a cold one unfulfilled.

Falling. Falling. Falling towards rapid eye movement his vision showed him a future.

She was barely moving. Had she been on her feet her knees both would be bent into angles. Her eyes both would be closed. Her arms stiff but angled as were knees. Her senses dulled to a near nilness. She was in a full heroin nod. One could place one's full flat hand on her posterior. Perhaps a minute or so later her mind may or her mind may not recognized and make a small body gesture of disobedience. She was in a full heroin nod. Her skirt loosely fitting and half, the top half of butt was fully uncovered. That she was either unaware of or could not cipher enough to rectify it, her heroine nod was in full form.

As he was beginning to comprehend what the vision was allowing his mind to see R. E. M. opened a window for the door to his vision had slammed tightly shut.

Eight hundred miles east a startled Milonya Trump held her arms riggedly outstretched. He bent legs muscles stealed and tight really little buttocks crammed closed and its usual soft spongy self hardened like rock.

Her head almost always as clear as a bell in the last two years went blank. She froze in a seventy eight degree room. Her swimming caught it. Years of practice with this woman since she a bit older than a toddler had not let miss any bodily action by her star aquatic student and hi board aerobatic diver. The two together had made Milonya a world class champion.

Everything went smoothly with the team except for that one hellish, horrific year when her champion-to-be lost her ever-loving-mind and fell for Herriberto. Herriberto Sanabria, that Puerto Rican, lousey fuk who somehow got her to put that damned spike in her arm.

General knowledge tells us a split second in the measurement of time only is fast. But like a limit in time there is no limit of what can and does happen in a split second.

A small child, a girl, fearless yet unknowing climbs an eight foot ladder about to attempt her first high dive. She has been well trained and well coached. That in her bikini swimwear is a vigilant guard in attendance at the pools edge where the diver still above is to make her submergence.

On the scene of the divers practice session is her publicity agent, M Rodney Paul Banks. Banks is a successful publish author. He has had fifteen of his books published.

In that same split second the diver froze he has had an enlightening joyous epiphany. That ought to get her he decided.

He was thinking of Morrell McCarrells, his second divorced wife.

I can let her catch me watching my three-d television shows while lying on the floor right under the screen. She's smart and will tell me stop trying to look under the dresses of females in the movie. She is that way. She could never keep that to herself. Away from me it has to hit her that I cannot see what's under the dresses of the televised females anyway, Idiot!!

But I'll keep letting her catch me doing it. I'll get her attention over and over. She probably will even throw her hands up in surrender. Still I'll keep her catch me at it.

Once I have her total attention, she'll start to peep around the corner before she passes by the projection room. That is when I'll be sure I have her. Banks count not help but smile. No facial expression though. None other than that one looking like the kitty that ate the aviary pet.

Then I'll abandon those actions and get my video recorder. Soon enough I will, said with conviction, catch her trying to lie on the floor to see if she could possibly have been wrong about what I may have seen lying there.

I can see her now taking out the three-d television three-d glasses. Checking-up on me.

That's where the cam- recorder comes in.

All that is necessary for this deviousness to be accomplished is I have to invent a pair of three-d television glasses.

Banks also was a successful inventor. The books made him a multiple deca millionaire. His three inventions made him a billionaire.

His hobby was arranging for his daughters futures they had chosen for they are reachable.

His oldest daughter's split- second of hesitation had ended and she began to spring the diving board.

He did again suppress that old feeling of fear. The one he had gotten that day. The day he had attended her practice. She was ten years and neither his daughter nor her diving trainer had thought to apprise him, to warn him of her next step in training that had been taught to her two months before that fateful day.

Two months earlier to that practice.

Now Liebshen for your next lesson. One that will serve you well. First. As all ways I would progress to this step should you not be ready to except. Normally when you dive you as I have taught you reach the depth of the pool to where the force of your dive expires and you arch your frame and approach the surface, and when your surface you take on air. It is the humane and the correct procedure. No?

Now that you are ready I will introduce to you a friend.

Once your body reaches the point to where your submergence no longer is forced into the pool you're the weight and your, dive, do not arch upward. Do not arch upward to reach the surface; rather kick your two legs. Go deeper into the water. Touch the bottom and push off the floor of the pool to gain momentum. Come to the surface and do not forget whom you had just such a short couple seconds ago shook hands with. My friend is the bottom of the pool? Replied her student. Ja, liebshen.

He had almost dived into the pool that day.

He had taken only two steps towards his daughter when he saw her surfacing. He was angry until she emerged and in a triumphant cry with both fist raised and total glee in her face. We did it!!, did he began to calm and see her training had progressed. His heart would still beat. Her mother would allow him entry again tonight he mused-somewhat. He had been the chooser of her coach and teacher.

Forward back to the present.

When practice was done he kissed her his usual I love you infinity on her forehead.

Before he left she went to the shower.

She and the coach left the gym and there the two of them were. Big as day. The billboard across the street from the gym's front door on three large poles it showed the phot of a man's back. He was well dressed. The backs of his celebrity boots polished to a patent leather gleam. His right forefinger cupped by a little hand. That hand attach to two and a half foot beauteous smile on her face turned to look behind her. She in patent leather flat footwear, ankle socks with lace, a flowered dress knee high and two pigtails with a negro league baseball cap turned around backwards. The billboard phot-shops a trip to the Bentley. Bentley is still an auto of prestige. The little girl is Menmeth, her little sister and the man had only a short period of time left her with in the gym's pool area with a I love you infinity smooth.

Only three hours past he had passed out from near exhaustion. He had three unrelated dreams in that time, neither had any things to do with the other two. He remembered none of them as soon as they ended. Fate on occasion is not fickle. He was soon to be awakened. He would soon see the face of one of the dreams main characters. The doorbell rang.

CHAPTER SIX

Lockdown, a phrase used by the occupants and authority figured from the top position, warden to the secretary who answered her phone calls.

Dallas Federal Penitentiary, a mid-level security penal institution had been locked down for seventy two hours.

In a prison lockdown no inmate or prisoner as some would is then was allowed to leave the cell. The shower and medical calls were the only exceptions.

There was one other exception. Lockdowns were supposed to prevent this one but on this day lockdown purpose was ineffectual.

Count was being made. There were two hundred six inmates in this block. Three guards made the count of the prisoners. Should there have been no lockdown only two guards were used.

As soon as count started in the very first cell where two inmates were incarcerated there was to be only one, as Brook Adams, in for a three to five bit on petty theft charges was the reason for the lock down. Adams along with three others doing time but from a different block on the prisons opposite side had been murdered while in the yard.

The count stopped at very first cell. Lying on the floor was Pervial Ambergarten Jones. Three puddles of blood lye under his body. Blood had gushed from the back of his head. His body flat and faced down had a larger puddle under his abdomen to his left side. The last and most prevalent of the pools of blood was settled from the soaked area of his crotch.

Connectional office Leonara Bentley went back to the hood were the on duty CO's office is. She sounded the alert for the Gorilla Squad.

And then she hit the medical alert. No physician in a case as this were allowed to enter an inmates sleeping area without the seven C.O. Gorilla Squad.

These are ones no one inmate wanted to fend off. They all were over six feet six inches tall. They all were over three hundred eighty five pounds. They all came with steel batons and steel toes boots. They all were merciless. As a group Warden Charlene Shirley gave them all the "go" signal. She stood behind them figuratively one hundred percent. She alone had handpicked them. Of course had she stood behind physically, then all of her four foot ten and one half inches in height and he one hundred one pound frame would be totally invisible. Also she was never without her American Eagle, fifteen shot hand gun nine millimeter.

One could easily but should never misjudge that soft skinned, soft smile, soft narrow lips cherub like angelic face. She would put a group of holes in one's head if she had even the slightest provocation. The biggest rumor on her was she had another nine in an ankle holster.

Follow procedure. I will be in forty five minutes. Charlene told her guests with apologies the night would have to end early, right this minute even.

Her six guests reclothed themselves. Two females pursed their assorted apparatus's. Gave their regretful sorrows. Said they were having a swell time and the fun loving socialite disappeared, in her place was a four star uniformed prison warden.

The last three things she did before approaching her Hummer in the garage was to holster her waist nine millimeter put on her left ankle desert eagle and lastly put on her right ankle desert eagle nine millimeter.

The garage door went up and humming H2 well out the electronic eye opened gate. She was gone.

On her way a curiosity struck her. The in Ukraine. Ukrainian Americans are sending Ukraine aide in supplies, money and have gone to Ukraine to fight against Russia. They are than in fact fighting to kill Russians, so what are the Russian Americans doing for their heritage country?

What will the American President do should Russian Americans fight against the ethnical war the American president has approved? Russians are Americans. Will he arrest them as the Japanese were during World War Two? And if he does, then how will that play.

Her Russian prisoners bleeped into her real of awareness.

Things were bad. They got even worse the next morning. She had showed in her office shower. The odor of the night before gave way to a hint at her personal. She needed to walk the prisons floor. Get a feel of what. All she knew was four murders had happened. One while in lockdown where no one could get a prisoner without the prisoner's cell door being unlocked. The prisoner also was in the cell alone. The next part she hated, it was a question. Two words only. The guards? Body smelling fresh and of lavender perfume she was about to press the intercom and order Zythe Mendell her secretary for this week to call up her body guards to escort. She was tough as pig-iron, but being smart as the process that turned coal to diamond she would not go alone. Plus it was prison procedure.

Her buzzer rang her first.

Deputy Warden Wallace on the line warden

Yes Wallace? Bad news! We have an escape.

CHAPTER SEVEN

Three days ago.

So the next few hours are going to bring one heck of an ice storm. This storm was totally unexpected. It should start in the next fifteen minutes to half an hour.

One hour later.

The news band glides across the television screen. The surprise ice storm that was supposed to happen did not form.

The next news band read, the body that was found in abandoned warehouse that was being rigged with explosives for implosion has been determined to be Frederick Glasni. His identity was found through dental exams and fingerprints.

The television program continued without further interruption.

A tear rolled out of an eye. Then another and another. By the time the fourth tear came both eyes began to run as two dripping faucets.

Three days later.

Whose missing asked the warden? The answer ran a chill through her. That same type of chill still clung to the deputy warden. Evan Glasni.

CHAPTER EIGHT

From the news of the dead body in the abandoned warehouse he made a phone call, that was yesterday.

The seven forty seven landed in Maple view. He had taken no luggage, only stuff his pockets with Franklin's and Grant's, a total of two hundred six thousand dollars.

The twenty BMW picked him up. Your weapons and ammo are in the truck when you are done dump this car. He knew that meant clean of any evidence that any one who had been in it would be identified.

He dropped the deliverer off and slowly rode out.

CHAPTER NINE

The police came late. There were broken table, pieces of wooden bar chairs, a hinge was buster it's top screws bent yet holding a hanging door. He had gone leaving those he asked of information who had denied him alive but sorry he took them on. He arrived in Maple view only an hour ago.

The restaurant owner gave the word to the two district officers a neighbor had called. This was a family squabble. Two brothers over one of their wives. The officers removed themselves reporting the 911 call unfounded and a couple hundred dollars a piece richer. The truth was he had gone to work seeking information on who it was that took the life away from the son of a friend. He was one of the boy's two godfather's.

The place looked organized. There were two sitting in chairs at outside tables there was food in front of each. It sat there for never an hour. The second floor window blinds moved occasionally but only a slit at each movement and always the same Venetian rib. He decided to ask only one of them. One on the inside. He went through the front door grabbed a bottle of way, paid for it and began an exit. At the front door pff, pfft. No more outside guards. Turning nine more pfft's then he quietly strode up the stairs.

The hallway on the second story had one door. It was open and he shot her right in her back into the spine just above her crack of her buttocks, "she went rigid. Her entire body locked and then hit the carpeted throw roglimply.

She answered the only question he had to ask. He chose to accept it pfft pfft, into her head and he split.

On the way from the front door he shot a glance at who looked to be inappropriately dressed for the style in that area, as was he, not a clue to his partner. The second godfather.

That very night their paths crossed one another again. Gunfire raged inside auto manufacturing plant. The plant was closed due to presidential order in the effort to contain the spread of the pandemic.

The meeting was called by the three major business organizations in the state. All were suspicious of the others doings in the murders that had happened in the last twenty four hours.

The meeting just started when numerous explosions were heard. The business startled guns appeared and roaring automatics begin riddling the plush office and some had time to seek cover from injury a couple took hits.

More explosions were heard. Again the booms heard were outside the manufacture plant. Their outside security was being blow apart. They thought treachery among themselves. This meeting had been immediately called profit was at stake.

Something had happen. The heads of the organizations sought ways to retreat to escape the flying cop killers. They had been hoping for their guards outside to enter and assist in their cowardly retreats. None of outside lookout, body guard henchmen were able to.

The ammunition inside was depleted.

Fear of death forced the sides to flee seven men of the twelve were alive and retreated. All three sides found their guards dead and every automobile decimated. Burning. They had to retreat on foot. The seven who ran in all directions were found dead. Gunned down. They were scattered. Investigation told they died in numerous spots. None closed the a football field's distance to one another.

The godfather found dead bodied that he had not finished off.

I have help. Each came to that conclusion.

In the message parlor and two thousand dollars out of his pocket and into the pardons cash register he had been lying still on his back half of his on the bed. His legs hanging over feet flat on the floor. He had fallen asleep almost as soon as he lied down.

The deal he had made with Mommasan was still being kept.

Her knees were on the folded comforter. She was totally nude. Totally engrossed in carmine her way. Her hair held back by the scrunchie. As she began to tire, so went deeper on him. Opening up wider because the deal was for her to not release him, so before going to sleep herself she also with her mouth engulfed his testicals along with his meat-rod. Secure should she sleep as she had the feeling she would the package would not escape her oral chamber. She shortly slumbered.

Going along Ben Gazzra Way, his attention was taken away from his present duty. There stood a little boy about nine perhaps ten years old. What caused him to stop and pull over to the curb was that look on her face. He had seen hundreds even thousands of times before.

As he got out of the rented roadster, he gave her the old ahem. No notice of it from her, so he gave her an even louder harrumph. That gave way to her and she turned he head towards his approach.

She once the three of them spoke to one another informed her that he was not a policeman, but rather a citizen who handle the child's plight.

She took him home and called up to an upstairs window. Bellamy opened it, she become and Bellamy came to the front door. He was standing in the shadows.

I'm going to the police. By the time I get back I want you gone or what you've been doing hero is gonna put your ass right in jail. What I been doing to Leeroy. He took step towards. She stepped back pulling the child along with her by the shoulder of his polo shirt. I ain't done shit to Leeroy he gritted. You have too, said the boy. Boy I ought tuh. She pulled her child a further away. Past the alleyway. Get out of my apartment she threaten said to him. Again she stepped back pulling little Leroy with then she feigned a turn suggesting the two would be on their.

Threatened he launched a himself towards their pretended retreat. Both she and the oy ridgedly flintched and she grabbed son and put up an arm to protect them from outstretched arm. He did reach them.

Instead a surprised child rapist and would be assaulted was forcefully yanked from behind off his feet into a dark alleyway between the two houses.

The noise of the attack did not last long, maybe fifteen seconds, then came pfft. Pfft. Pfft. The black small figured mother made a correct assumption a silencer from a pistol had just gone off.

The stranger emerged from his dark hideout. Your problems are over. He kneeled in front of the boy. Never allow that to happen to you without telling your mother to call the police and report it. We have men doing jail time and some of the prison police who will handle such types of people. He looked in the mother's eyes. She looked into his, as he said to the boy. Promise me. Leroy gave his promise.

The no longer a complete stranger to them began to stand straight but in a crouch he remembered the fullness of the routine, and Leroy, he said softly yet solemnly you are never to do that to a child, boy or girl. Become a MGA, a good and get you a woman. An adult for your exploits. Promise me. I promise.

Then he became erect. The woman held onto the forearm she had latched herself to and guided him upstairs. He, the man had taken awareness that she had peered into the alleyway while he took the oaths from her son and saw the offensive boy could not be seen.

To the woman and her child the world just got a retrieval.

CHAPTER TEN

The shuttle according to the National Aviation Space Administration reports the Air Force Quest launch last week while testing its new hyper speed coil performed to well. For greater than anticipated. When set in launch it was supposed to richocette around the planet Mars then be shut down and rendezvous with the Russian controlled International space station.

When launched it went into a speed not anticipated and in less then three minutes left our solar system and in a half hour has departed from out Milky Way Galaxy.

It is confirmed too that all of Earth's tracking satellites have lost communication and there has been no contact.

We switch now to Mac Humper is Spain where the communication was recorded.

The biggest news story in history and the couple never heard a word a word from the set. The child who had been rushed off to bed to give his mother and her newly found protector a bit of space for him to accept her appreciative... stood in his partially opened bedroom door and viewed the news broadcast.

Her bedroom door had closed for over an hour. He could not have heard even if the bedroom door had been left open. Her thighs covered and nullified all sound from both of his ears.

Both god fathers had been in the same condition until daybreak the next morning.

That day break brought on his departure the television still on had a commercial that gripped him into a momentary stillness.

The governor of the state stood there on the screen. Four uniformed police officers stood silently in still motion.

Thank you. Said the governor for allowing my bill to become law. Now no child or child's parent have any reason not to bring the molester and in some cases molesters of a child whether uncle, aunt, any other family member or a parents live-in mate to get away with breaking the law of child molestation. There is now no statute of limitations on the crime of child molestation. We take credit for this legal action. Yet we give credit to a governor in the state of Pennsylvania for the attempt, though it to date has been only an attempt to raise the age of the molested victim to be raised from their own age of thirty five too the age of fifty as an age was his proposed statue of limitations in that state.

That was a good thing the god father said to the woman he was about to leave. Yeah. That commercial has been ordered by our governor to come on at least once a day everyday and at various times. He said in his first one he wanted to get the message to all of us. That one was on three or four times a day for about three months until he got his bill made into a law.

Crazy thing those commercials were paid for by the top ten businesses in the country. She kissed his neck with her flicking tongue and both hands on his panted crotch.

Still he had work to do.

Just hours later a news update told of a center city business district's traffic being detoured. A well multimillionaire and owner of tallest building in the had been murdered. He was found on the entrance way to his buildings private parking lot. His head had been blown from his neck. Presumably the weapon was a shotgun. His chauffer been shot in his forehead through the limo's front windshield. There were no witnesses. More at ten.

The business just yesterday had been freed on bail of seven hundred fifty thousand dollar cash bail. He had been arrested on the charge of child sex trafficking.

When the on scene criminologist was allowed to view the crime scene he munerted a hint of soy sauce was in the air. None was discovered on any physical surface. The aroma would linger and present itself here and there at times to come.

His cell he had kept on. WKBW radio station out of Buffalo New York still broadcast in these days. As it should be.

It was the most talked radio show of all time back in the day. Back in the day he caught himself. That day my moms was only three years old. Her folks, probably had her hacker in that late at night. Smiling. At least she got to see the Jean Peters, Gene Barry movie war of the worlds based on that back in her day radio show. Hmph. Base or the HG Wells book. Those thoughts went so quickly he had more time less at the stop traffic light to tune in his download of the radio program remake on his phone. The only cause he ever kept his phone on when doing a job.

Ladies and gentlemen, this is Dan Neverette, the program began.

Again a smile. Though Dan Neverette had died years back his son carried on his memory of that self same radio broadcast remake.

She was going to make him breakfast before he pulled up. Instead he left twenty Grants on her kitchen table. The alnight pharmacy. He pulled over. Toothpaste, toothbrush, dental floss, mouth wash and a bottle of water.

Behting wat, is my choice. Belting War it is. Now for the last detail but a poignant one. Should you care for floral arrangements we will need your specification. Type, color and quantity. The customer held her words. She did however take note of the funeral parlor's director's use of arrangements rather than arrangement, her use of the word quantity being suggestive of more than what could be used and or should be used. She kept to being calm though her seething rage mounted. She had to hold the woman only doing he job. She was doing what she is paid to do. She was only working on providing for her family as she herself has, had always done. Not anymore, her son's dead. She had no more family. Her line was ending with her. The funeral directory had not done this this thing to her. If only his father were here in stead of. If his were not in prison. If only you were here.

At the funeral arrangement meetings end the cost was paid in cash. Forty six thousand nine dollars eight cents.

She a thirty female counted the eight cents out first. True this is payment for her only child's funeral. Still may as well hold onto as much money as long as she could.

Mackenna Johnsen walked her to her car. He kissed her and hugged her. You going to be alright getting home hon? Sure I just want to sit here for a minute. Johnsen waited until she felt able to drive safely then he got on his Harley and went back to his office.

Benjamin Franklin middle school has a young slender Asian science labs teacher. He has died his hair a different color each in the reasoning students would physical and chemical change with the coloring of is defiantly. A visual teaching aid.

Twenty six students around bunson burners acids and other materials forces his attentions to be its highest at all times in the laboratory.

He pays very close attention to all of his students in all of his classes. Today he had taken note that Bobby, his given name, Robert Guess, is not only paying acute attention in class but for the only time to date four months plus into the school years is without prod participating in class.

He has summised but holds it no steady solution that his home abusal must have ended. He is right in his summization. The abuse has stopped. Tonight in the teachers home while lounging he will find the child's antagonist has been murdered. However he will not know if for sure and he will not associate the two.

CHAPTER ELEVEN

Even Glasni held court hundred times in his earlier years. Only once had he found his prey he was paid to assign a penalty of death did he not allow execute the sentence. He was well know by his fifth year in business. That one time he hid his face from his prey he found no fault in the boy and executed the payee of the hit.

Some only a sparsity tried to call him fair. Truth was fair had nothing to due with him changing the sentence. The boys father paid Glasni ten times the amount Glasni had been paid to cancel the young sprites life.

Even Glasni twenty years to arrest on any charge. Problem was his only arrest resulted in a ten years sentence. In his year he walked out. He could have within his first six months. He had figured out how.

The news broadcasted the finding of a dead body in abandoned warehouse. He paid little attention, hardly enough to give it a thought later that same day.

Hey Glasni, Pondurance a, lifer times three called to him as Glasni's cell was being passed. Pondurance had faked an illness. He was hoping to leave with Glasni.

Yeah Glasni answered. I know you get a plan on how to get outta here. I'll pay you my debt you take me with you.

I am not leaving for another two if I keep out of trouble Pondu, but yes you are right if I chose to leave out of here I do have a way. He was surprised. Pondurance would know that much about him. Even with his convictions Pondu as Glasni, called him, not many dared to, was a wise guy. Crooked Nosed, you understand.

Even though some scum sucker killed yo kid?

What are talking of Pondurance? Your kid they found him dead in an empty warehouse. Been on the TV all day.

CHAPTER TWELVE

The escape of Glasni hit the aire. There was evidence on how he had gotten out of the medium secure prison. His escape took a backseat to report that he had escaped at the same time as the life times sentence Elipse Pondurance a well known organized crime hitman.

The search was on for Pondurance and Glasni.

It was reported that Glasni's son had recently been found dead and televised and that that broadcast is more than likely to have made Glasni and model prisoner until the newscast assist Pondurance in his escape.

Mrs. Hennie Yun was the wife of Ji Li Yun, a purveyor of automatic, semi-automatic hand guns and shot guns. He was the owner of his shop Yun Weapons. Yun arrived at shop, it was already open as usual. Yun employed two people at each of his two hundred Yun Weapons worldwide dealerships.

Meazzy Smythe an Eglishter as Cole Partar called his origin was the senior of the two employees.

Good morning sir said Smythe. Good morning boss said Partar. Good morning guys Yun returned. Everything okay here? Asked you. The usual Smythe came back with.

Yun's office phone rang. It Jeet Kun Yun, the oldest son named after the art of self defense developed by a legendary Chinese Kung fu master.

The conversation went on casually but before it ended Jeet said to his dad I talked to you for a while very casually because I was ordered to do so. I am on speaker. We are being held as hostages. This is want our captors want from you.

Then a strange voice came over his houses land line. That's all I require. As soon as you bring them to me your family and you are free from this.

Mezzy you guys can leave an hour so early today. Cole I need you to secure a couple of items.

Yun and Cole went into the store room. Yun gave Cole a short list. I'll need these at eleven fifteen. Cole surveyed the list. You got boss. It was ten thirty, close to anyway.

Three thirty PM the gun shop closed.

Two hours earlier the police sent a detective and three uniformed officers, one of them the field supervisor were in the Yun household.

The supervisor held the rank of corporal. He in ranking outranked the detective and had charge of this ongoing case if he chose to.

He had my family as hostages. You better believe I gave him what he wanted. If you love your family, you do the same.

I am not arguing with you Mr. Yun. Nor am I saying you did anything wrong. Just putting down what you and your family tell me.

All you gave to him was three sets of guns. All three fifty seven magnum with interchangeable barrels. Those barrels were twelve, ten, eight, six and four inch barrels. Also each of the three sets had all those interchangeable barrels in each set. You also gave him the tool kits to change the barrels, each changing kit came with each magnum set. Lastly the ammunition was ten cases, forty shots per case, all the ammunition was Teflon coated. Have I got the list correct? Yes. But he also had me give him two dragon scale vest. Bullet proof. I'll make sure I put that down.

The detective asked the supervisor, you got anything to ask that may help us here? You're on point.

Glasni was gone. He had kept to the script that kept him from prison for so many years. Three pair of surgical gloves. Face mask. Athletic mouth protector. No finger prints. No facial recognition. Verbal disguise. The other measure(s) are top secret. He was gone clean.

The kidnapping did not remove the two escaped prisoners from the news TV screen completely but it did cut down their usual two or three minutes a day down to thirty seconds two or three times a day.

Glasni slept on the pavement outside of an all filled shelter for the homeless. He kept to himself. But the billboard directly across the street held off his sleep for hours. He did not know why the ad disturbed him so much. Could his son have been raped too along with being murder and discarded in such a manner?

Has your child been raped? In big red letters on a white billboard. At the middle of the ad. Turn in the rapist even if it is a family member or your, sex, partner, was put in the ad under, loved one, that a line was drawn threw.

At the bottom was inked, either you or the rapist is going to get busted. Save the babies!!

He must have been only half unconscious in his sleep because not wanting to be identified he covered his face each turn.

CHAPTER THIRTEEN

The godfather were equally like minded. Though one got the news of Glasni's freedom hours before the other. Each in turn within seconds of the news knew. Both thought the exact same two word phrase. He's here.

They knew of Glasni. Glasni did not know they were in town.

Glasni was pretty sure no one other than he knew the two of them knew him. No one alive knew the two were his son's grandfather's, so once there since he could not contact the young man's mother for information. The feds were sure to on the look out for him here. He called Jason Jatum. No answer. Then he called thee Bundy. No answer. A second of concern. The television news report hit him. I saw it. They are here. Three bulbs now burned bright. Like there tempers they all burned hot with hatred. If the s-o-b's weren't dead already than they soon would be.

Hello Miss. May I ask you one question. My son was just buried. I know. That is why I flew twenty five hundred miles. Slightly confused and suspicious but no questions. I am here because his father would want me to be here. I don't know you and his father's in prison, so do not lie to me. Ma'am. I am you son's godfather. His father is no longer in prison. G, broke out last.

A few feet away a stranger stood still and quiet and thinking of clacking open a skull. The second godfather still held his stand. His mind heard. His mind went into attack mode. Then his mind thought, he's here.

I will get in touch with you soon. Even would want me to help out with you expenses. Please except this. The ten grand was in a yellow business envelope. He decided then and there. See if I can trust her. When you even, say I said hello. Say I stopped in and gave my respect. He walked away. The Corvette door had closed. He would not have heard her call out and ask what his name was except the Vet's drop-top was folded away. He pointed the envelope and left.

Repat Roera, is the greatest written of short storied in this century. His books have sold over three quarter billion copies in the past eleven years. The have yielded nine big screen motion pictures grossing six billion dollars over all. Some of his characters have been made into action figures with accessories and again yielding in the deca-billion dollar range.

Today his release from state prison is being televised. All of his novels were written while he was the guest of the prison system in the Republic of Brazil.

He owes no time to the government as far as parole. He did do all of his time he was sentenced to. He in convict terms, maxed out.

Mevat Lashist is there to greet him at his arrangement. Lashist is the highest charging and most successful prostitute in South America.

They immediately process by chauffer driven Bentley limo to the airport and the private he has arranged to take them to North America.

His youngest nephew of seven years of age had been getting sexually molested. He has a need to comfort his sister, talk to his nephew and appease North America of the breathing of air of childhood rapists, since the laws in America do not cover the spectrum of his sister's complaints.

One the jet. Ahhh. Regular eats.

Fresh clothing. Citilian gators. Electric razor. Platinum, white jade and rhinestone, rings watch, bracelet and neck chain, all he adorned after he and Mevat took care of the natural calls of one released from an all male prison over a long period. This was mainly to allow Mevat to believe she was doing an astronomical deed. Reality had shown since his writings in his second year of incarceration had made him not only a star but a rich star the female guards had been earning a thousand dollars two or three times every week.

Through those satiated years he held to one desire. He added it to his to do list. Once this trips business is concluded he will return to Brazil to seek an affair with both the wardens and assistant warden's wives.

His mind was a bit perturbed. His release a couple minutes ago could Mevat have caused that one?

The thought he held in his mind. What do those wives look like? That inquiry stabbed at his brain over and over. Perhaps to get ease of mind is why he chose to have the auto's chauffer pull over in order that might find the reason for the gathering of people listening to the high yellow complexioned speaker on the podium. He had no reason to do so. His sister and nephew were the direction he was traveling, yet he stopped. He listened. He heard.

The speaker barely took notice of the two seeking his message that had just exited the Bugati.

Speech continued and the only in the car with J.F.K. in the back seat was his at that time wife Jackie B. Kennedy. On the thirty foot high projection screen used for showing movies outdoors showed the reason for his opinion.

As the former president's head rest on his chest from being shot in the back of his head, his at that time wife Jackie turns sideways towards him places her left hand under his chin resting on his chest and pieces of flesh, brain and the top of his skull bone burst upward into the air. Quickly as though from force his head is flung upward and backward.

The only way this could have happened by gunshot wound as reported the second shot did to him is if Jackie Kennedy had the apparatus that fired that second shot. The video of the assassination shows it plainly. Why then if I realized it, and you can see did the Central Intelligence Agency not pick it up. Its right there in front of our eyes. That is why I had the movie stopped where our former president was shot both times?

I will not pause here because there is more to see. As the video progressed with a later pointer he showed the assassinated president's wife crawing out of the back of the car where the president was assa- no I am going to interject murdered here where she comes in contact with what was supposed to be secret service agent who was at that point on top of the trunk of the president's transport.

Here again the video stops showing Jackie and a reported SS agent both on the car's trunk. Then it is played on to see the agent get off the car and leaves. The wife of the president calmly gets back into the back seat of the car. Where by the way the president has just been murdered. Why?

Why did the SS agent not take her away from area being shot into as if he knew she would be safe?

Ladies, gentlemen, citizens I leave you with this. That assassination, murdering a president of the United States of America was over fifty years ago. To this date no one who saw what you just saw and being in position to right our children wrongly taught nor even attempt to bring the governmental guilty to trial. Why?

You saw it. I saw it. This is our country. Why are we powerless to do so?

The couple took glances around. Then with urging, a slight urge from Roera, Mevat leaves with him to re-enters the Bentley.

CHAPTER FOURTEEN

Are you one of superstitious values? I myself am not. Still for this book I will not put to paper the reputational unlucky number thirteen. To be blunt, no chapter thirteen will ever by my own hand be in this publication.

The Friar was a new man to him. One he had not been in the past acquainted with. His former life is why he approach the Franciscan. Mass had ended and as Friar Joseph Mole, was leaving the room above the food distribution located over the offices on the floor below in order to head to his living quarters across the street on the even ending number of the block where he would come out of his duty robe a man he had never met, yet- he seemed so similar.

Friar, he spoke to the priest, may I have a solemn few words with you?

I see no reason not to. Is it immediately important? Or, can you wait about ten minutes while I go home and change? Realizing the stranger and her had never met, I live right across the street. Faher it is important. I hope it may take only a few minutes. Please? Shoot your breeze says friar mole.

This will have to be in the order of a confession. Okay? The priest says his few words of assurance.

Before you tell me, I do recognize you. I saw your phot on the free neighborhood paper.

Good. My confession will not take so long. I have escaped prison for a reason. I am here to find out who murdered my boy. Don't know if he made that paper but a couple days ago he was found dead in the old abandoned candy warehouse. I saw it on the news after an inmate told me. I am going to kill who did it. That is my confession. Please say a prayer for my son and is mother and for me.

I was going to do my time and come home father but now...

Blessing are given except for the part of the intentional murder. That was explained. The two parted ways.

CHAPTER FIFTEEN

We look like this. Thanks for registering in your own name. It made it easy to find you. You come across any news for me? You find out yet who took my kid out?

You know I got busy soon as I heard. Munch, the boy's nickname, got real lucky having two godfathers. Yeah. I figured if either of you got his, he would someone to look out after him. Figured I would need the – hey both of you here? Seen him taking to Munch's mom. Introduced himself to her. Trying to get info I guess. Don't think he did.

Think we should go get him? No. That train wrecker is a stone cold loner. Dependable as day and night, twice as loyal and four times deadlier than he is loyal. Just like you, if he finds out who did that he'll go home. He finds out I broke out he will stay away from my family.

I'm tired of talking lets move man. This may be your home town, but I say we paint its sky bloody til munch's murderer is in the dirt. Good move. Let's go.

The two went in different directions.

Leaving the monk. Robert Orton. Killed your boy entered his mind. The message was received in his mind as a truth. He knew that such notations were sent out to a person. On most such occasions the person the cipher was sent to was also admitted to others brain receptors. One usually did not know who else was delivered.

He kept his reply of gratitude for after verification.

This being an escaped prisoner was awkward to him. None of his known contacts could be used.

The forty five godfather number one had given him accompanied only two full clips outside of the one loaded into the grip of the gun his shirt completely camouflaged. He had surprised his backup so no other arrangements were set to get more. Basically this city, his city was a nude baby he had just met.

Later that night while talking to God Friar Robert Orton says to God, in my own heart I must confess I wish to tell convicted criminal who has escaped from prison on the only purpose of the taking away the life of the man who murdered his son even though he unlike myself does not yet know who raped and murdered the boy. Both men told me of their lives. One past and one future. You will intercede and see to it that justice is done? That was the question of the night.

Your word demands the rapist death via man to boy. May lying man as he does with woman is an sin punishable by death. The father by your law has the right to put the sodoniser to death and I cannot tell the father because I learned of the abomination in the confession. Sanity must abide.

You put something in my way, so should I put to death the abominable sinner, will you still go up to the deed with me?

After that talk the monk desired some fresh air and Molly White pulled closer to the cemented walls surrounding the entrance to the house two doorways down the block. The man who had been walking the through the area looking for a quickly found her easily. He looked out while she stooping gave a half-ass performance. The friar was not new to this neighborhood. The two years since he had been transferred here from Philadelphia, Mississippi showed him that drug addled areas and hookers have mush in common.

The guy Molly was per scoping with has what the hung like a horse group would call a embryo sized dick. That aspect of his body was not an odd thing with one exception. His biological father was one of those guys with a very big cock. You would say his father a hung like a horse group. His tiny four and a half inch stiffy was a trait of the males on his mother's side.

His father on the birth of his son was a ninety nine plus percent positive the two were father and son. Molly swallowed his member fully with a laughable ease.

Since he paid he a hundred dollars she did not come off of it until his ejaculation and both departed happily. He back home to regret his miserable living single existence bring alone again. She directly to her peoples crack house slash shooting gallery and called out to Brooklyn the neigh hood crack dealer on that four to midnight shift.

Ahh. The night air felt refreshing. On his way to the all night seven Twelve, a rip off of the major food chain store he saw Brooklyn handing out a couple of samples.

The monk had seen the scene in all of the Ghetto areas in all the major minority areas in all the cities he had been assigned and to date he could not fathom the truth why illegal drug sales exist. The police had in all those places bee aware of the illegality and the illegal law breakers on both sides pushers and buyers.

Some day he tried to think. The law will do its job fully. He prayed to God for forgiveness for thinking a false witness.

Lunch proved to be as unsucculent as a flat tire. Do not blame the service not blame the cook. The service usually good became excellent. The matribee recognized her. He told the waitress whose table the women would be seated. You see that woman in the pink tight slacks that was said. Not spoken as a question. She is the mother of the kid found dead in the candy plant. I saw her on the news. Be at your absolute best. A message went to the chef. Do this order especially right. Everything precisely as ordered. The know Clemonton. Clemonto Morgosi, the matridee got the okay from is staff. So the service was polite to the point of being curtious beyond expectations. The food was the best ever served.

The mood of a mother's grief not yet sedated was at it's fulfillment. The meals were barely touched. Perhaps if the four females had known what the restaurant's workers had done to please them and to ease a mother's torment, then maybe the meal could have the detecting taste buds.

Two went to the lavatory to remove the shine from their noses. Although I never did know a few snoots of cocaine dust was how a proboscis was rendered an outbreak to dullness.

The mother told a third to go back to the car. She had forgotten something and needed it. The third female tiny tittiel, scrawny legged, very thin arms, thick unattractive eye glasses had a posterior the size of which would fat, fat woman envious. It was so huge then when she had sat down half or more spilled of the dinner tables chair seat.

The mother alone with the last one gave her a few words not seeing anger nor gleam from either of the ladies. The group let a total of two hundred in gratuity.

CHAPTER SIXTEEN

The entire country got the news and were in shock. When he escaped from prison as a hit man for organized crime nine out of ten people interviewed swore their opinion was he would be in an a extradition treaty country. He would only return to the US if a hit was ordered.

He had committed suicide late at night when cornered by the FBI. That type of suicide had become common in the latter years. Mostly for cop killers. Mostly.

The other story was the law no one knew was being pushed through by the Federal Transportation Advisory Board. It passed with only descending vote.

This law will make air travel more difficult for drug users and safer for all airline passengers and employees.

Test would be given to all passengers before boarding. The test is for illegal drug use. If a passenger or employee's test came up positive the user would be arrested immediately when the plane lands. The charge would be a felony. Illegal possession of narcotics.

FBI local office. So it's decided we have put the team was on our dead fugitive in charge of your fugitive. They got their man first, so as agreed they are on the jet landing right about now. Co-operate when they get here.

Chief inspector no contact has been made with his family or people he knew. Its been two weeks since he broke out. I know his kid being murdered set him off. He did not make the funeral parlor before the funeral, nor the viewing, nor the burial. His most likely going to stay away from here and a year or so from now he will make a mistake.

Chief I got a feeling he's here now. All he wants is to get perp who got his boy. The boys friends are under surveillance.

Then we have nothing yet. I think I will bring the new officers into this and request we keep a closer watch on the schools they went to. What about the kids girl friend? He had two. They apparently do not know one another not even about each other being the other.

Chief do we have any more news on the pedifities registered in the area. Since the boy was raped, I still think that is the best group to follow-up on.

He hasn't been to the morgue either, I think Harry and Thomas are on their shift now. You think? You know Harry sir, if he came up with something. Check!

That is it gentlemen and ladies.

A knock on the conference room too. A well dressed female agent's head pokes through the door. She gets an okay from Chief Agent Bifrost.

He got him chief. Questioning look crosses Bifrosts brow. It is in his eyes also.

The case you're meeting on. The boy's rapist. A one hundred percent match from both the anal semen and his oral swabs. The perps name is, Molasses Arigon. Lives right here.

He is in custody. Precinct One. Alert them. Agent Rivers and Agent Mendletown will be there. Tell them do not transport him until after we interrogate him. Yes sir.

The very serious men met unscheduled outside of a police district and left out of it before the arrival of the FBI agents sent to be sure the prisoner was exactly what he was arrested for being.

The Feds walked inside the entrance went to the bullet proof glass window to show their identification and got enlightened. The police behind the glass in the office were unconscious.

Agent Mendletown picked the door. Everyone in the precinct was unconscious. They found the prisoner they had arrived in interrogate gone.

Somewhere across the Big Pond in England a security leak flows like olive oil around the planet. Curiously the leak comes in the form of a voice not unlike that of the Queen Mother. Nick, the voice goes, make sure our veterans are never mistreated in any manner. Those American veterans have been so distastefully miscared for by their Philadelphia Pennsylvania Regional office having their livelihood stolen by that regional office and their Congress, Senate and house of representation have done nothing to rectify the financial instability. Perhaps we should not directly say so to the world's public but I have made a decision to hit their government in the side of the face with a slush ball. Make sure the statement I prepared personally gets publicity. We of England are appalled at ourselves and heartfelt fully apologize for the act of slavery.

Make certain my forces are never treated so woefully as those veterans in the states.

The apology for slavery was broadcast worldwide but only South America was mention in the apology. You go girl.

That is what was the RV as the three tortured their captive. Never finding any reason, only that a female prostrated herself to have him do so.

Just before the prisoner was given a penectomy he gave them her name and place of employment. Then he was castrated his eyes gouged from their homes and his tongue after being cut out was violently shoved into his anus pore to block the seepage of alcohom and lighter fluid. The RV was doused fully with ten gallons of jet fuel and they left with it and him inside. A full blaze.

It was all over now. He did visit his son's mother. He did not visit his son's grave. He chose two very important mauvevers. Do not out her in the spot where she had to turn him in or be arrested herself. The second was as the first do not get caught. There work here done and all three now familiar with each other never saw one another again.

The reason starts in the next chapter.

CHAPTER SEVENTEEN

Four months three weeks five days six hours seven minutes eight seconds and one zeposecond from the date and time a three fifty seven hollow point went into the left eye of, Bitty Parker Schram, Longbow Scalper Riversend stepped off the passenger ladder of the Red bird seven fifty seven.

His tour in the Bolivian jungle ended in near disaster yet successful by the slimmest of margin.

He was given the news, old as it was that his son was dead, mutilated and burned to the point that one charred barely recognizable bone shard and ash remained.

That self same instant in time the President of the United States of America being on a state wide capital tour had just seconds before bit into a Nathanial's Chili dog with raw onions and mustard on a pretzel dough hot dog roll keeled over dead.

Starting to hail the next taxi cab in line, he was halted by a small hand placed fat on his bottom.

He was warmly in comfort where before the touch his heart eyes demeanor were as cold as dry ice.

Little Pearl, he quietly spoke with a loving tone that can easily be described as awesome.

He turned and she would have been there standing but Little Pearl Thunder storm the Saint Joseph's School for Lakota Apache orphaned children's owner was totally in love with Longbow Riversend and as he turned to see her she was already in the you looked on me mode and had lepy into the air wrapping her short arms around his neck. Her legs wrapped around his massive body and her lips were immediately accepted by his. The two were in love with each other over twenty years. She had a bond psychicly with him like no others on this planet. Where ever he was, whatever he did she always knew, even before the two first laid eyes on one another. She laid him that same day.

Her light heartedness assured him things were good.

The two walked to the parking area where her brand new fully equipped totally tricked out pink and white Hummer awaited. He drove.

Your equipment is in the back seat. One peace pipe. One torch. One piece of pipe. Let's go to the hotel first? There was the chance that Little Pearl had been with some other while he was away but it was not with me as he thought. He waited until a signal light caught them. While awaiting the color change her medium sized left full breast was in his palm was kissed through her blouse.

To the rental the went.

Baby that was good and I figured I better some fast. How soon you going to leave. Its just that you just got back. I sure would like more home time but for some reason I have been feeling you have a reason to not come home.

You here on the news about the boy that got found her in a candy company's closed building. No, I don't think so. I heard the news was on for days. Oh, yeah maybe this will ring a bell. The child's mother a week later was murdered. Shot in her eye outside of her job. She was a clerk in this city's capital building. She was the boys mother, yeah I remember that. There is no easy way to tell you. The woman was on assignment with me. The kid was my son. No way I could lie to.

He never got to finish that sentence. She grabbed her truck keys and left as she went out of the door she gathered her clothing. Her panties, bra and tennis shoes she put on in the hallway after she closed the suite's door.

CHAPTER EIGHTEEN

Call off the troops. We found the killer. He's in pieces. Our perp is gone. He's not dumb.

In a loaned auto while at the stop light he lowered his window. The woman who had trapped on the windshield showed him the note written by his departed son's mother. He unlocked the passenger door and the woman got in.

She said to tell you one word. Enjoy. Then the oralling began with a red sheet covering her from head too the bottom of her flats.

The two left the city.

No one knew it but a stretch limo left the Nevada dessert and drove on into New Mexico. The driver drove into the dessert with a half full bottle of rose eighteen proof wine a black woman on his neck; fingers at the end of the ride his full blooded Lakota pecker.

Done was the first part of his revenge wrought for his dismembered son.

The second part done. He drove out of the dessert alone. The escaped criminals son's mom left behind, gutted.

Now to find the two god fathers and the father who shot his ex in her eye.

The news report came over the radio. There are still no leads to who was behind the president's assassination. China, Russia, Columbia, Zimbabwe and Afghanistan have all made speeches that the people are now better off. They have all refused to send any condolences.

This is Hal Crossfire and I say let this station take on all bets and cover any amount that this government is going to cover it up. And we all know why.

Again this is Hal Crossfire and that's the news for tonight. Tune in when we come back at nine p.m. good night.

Two months later the boarders on the north and coast lines were now not as severely guarded. The president's assassin had not be apprehended. This assassin would never be solved in the eyes of the public. This time unlike Kennedy's all of culprits would remain uncaught and unpunished.

There was some scattered chatter that loosening the boarder lines strangle hold would free a way to allow the assassin to escape. The people in the know had anticipated it and knew it would amount to zilch.

A phone call did come into the US Mexico border portal headquarters in Washington DC that twenty year old ice cream truck should only be a would be boarding crossing.

The call came from Washington DC Itself, so there was little attention being paid to it, but the law stated should a boarded crossing lead come in pass it on directly. The call proved fruitful. In the ice cream truck's freezer were Glasni's remains.

The escaped prisoner was dismembering, eyes gouged out and tongue shoved up the crispy blackened corpses an spore.

Needless to say the truck leaving Mexico was convescated.

When the news casted the fate of former escape, the call came into Washington, DC's boarder Patrol Headquarters that the driver was paid to transport the truck and body with his full knowledge he was transporting a dead escaped American prisoner and that he knew the patrol would be tripped off. Further a taped audio recording was sent to the largest Washington news paper. The Mexican was set free only after a month long investigation, including personal visits to his family and neighbors in Juan Chupa, his home communities suburb. He was clean and his bank account had only a five hundred dollar deposit two weeks before his trek into the US prison system. One day later Joseph O'brian Pesci walked into his apartment. Pushing the first button to shout off his alarm he took full awareness the unarmed white light bulb was already on. Two seconds later he alerted his body be aware. A millisecond later his eyes closed.

No Excedrin awaited him upon his consciousness arousal. What did await him brought fear to accompany the aching earing, head bell clanging pain that came from the Johnson bar's crash against his cracked skull.

He was on his knees and forearms tied tightly and his chest and stomach uncomfortable over a metal beer keg.

A voice came. Do not talk until I finish asking you, so you know exactly what I want and how your answer determines how this little scene will play out.

Family maybe special to you, but choices sometimes need to be made. Here is a choice you will make in ten seconds. Your brother's where abouts or yours and you kids in your graves within three days. I will leave your if you choose the wrong answer wife alive to fuck her brains out after you and her kids are dead.

Before leaving Sheryl Lym Bey was allowed to leave the bed room. He had backoned her and Alonzo her four year old son.

Fear was in his eyes as the two stood before his eyes. She showed him a hand mirror and he realized he was naked. In her had was a small steal bladed hachet.

She and Alonzo walked behind him Tape was then put over his mouth while the little boy instructed by his mother took six swings and chopped of his privates. A child is involved here, so privates are written of in the stead of –c- and ---i-.

The two went on and the hatchet left with his assailent chopped off his head.

Riversend made sure no fingerprints were left opened, left, closed the door and headed for Blend, Montana.

CHAPTER NINETEEN

What do you need us to do? Nothing. The line went silent. At least he's still alive. Now put him out of your mind until he's finished. You are alert right now. But only in the event he goes too far. You got it?

If you ring me, um not to hesitate.

Right. So far he's just off the grid. We know why, so we're not pushing at him. At not now. That's it. See you later. You too.

Tiger Li Jung had been given their orders.

Skip. We're not going to get any new missions until he's back in the fold? Most likely, but as I'll do, stay sharp, skip line went dead, the rest pusher their end call button.

CHAPTER TWENTY

Einez Bevery was having a little world with him. She had finally caught up to him in front of Manns, restaurant. The porkish looking Japanese female he arrived there with did of an arrogant bitchlike stare towards her, but the interruption was done with dignity and an utmost polite posture. She still struck a leer towards the intruder.

I know of someone in need of your special skills continued Einez. Please allow only a few minutes of your precious attentiveness.

Ling, please go to the table. I promise I will be in shortly. Ling Mu Ling conceded and the greeter gave her the table exactly as she ordered.

The conversation ended, and they're holding her fourteen year old until she makes them money enough to let her have her freedom. Those crackheads are never going to hold onto what they force her to make. You can win a large wages her child will be doing the same things they have her mother doing.

Names and some suspected addresses were given to him. Departure led her again to the federal Bureau of Investigation and he to Ling Mu Ling.

Found but a setting displeasing to launch his revenge. So close, so close, so close.

She still had a bit of eel morsel between her grinders. On the way to the taxi barn she kept tasting it. She had that opportunity to such it out or crab a minty toothpick. She chose the flavor.

The taxi driver never got out to let them in. He opened the door for her entry. Her panties exposed while her legs parted as she entered. The shock took hold of her immediately. She froze while her legs were still apart. The driver got a good long gander of a thing thong exposing a left vaginal lip.

He was a bit startled she left her legs open to that exposure. Further when he took a look why she was not being corrected. The body of her date started sliding to the sidewall. The whole was almost four inched across his forehead. Death so quick his face was not even showing a surprised. No statement except from the driver as the corpse hit the ground.

This one he did not care to hide. The news should have his last quarry aware he was the last of the three removing all the doubt why Glasni was found in pieces.

What he did not know is he was already being hunted. Usual in a hunt there is a prey. Not this time.

He was not sure but just in case, he kept his eyes wide open. He knew only a dunce could not realize his end pointed towards nearness. He knew where to wait. He chose a fling. He kept his head on two methods of death. Poison and explosives.

The first class flight still would not expose him. He had to expose himself.

It was long ago. The insurance company paid the full life insurance policy. Three quarters of a million dollars.

Already upper middle class she never changed her address. She had become easy to find.

The woman, a stranger to her followed her during the day. With the quietness of a butterfly the woman slept in her home while she slept without her knowledge.

When she went out Clichet, his allonym and Broken Arrow, his allonym stayed in her home without her knowledge.

Ben Neck, his allonym kept watch in shifts with Allnym, his allonym aw snipers. Even their own squad members could not see them. They were that good.

When this third godfather was to make a play it would not play.

His plain lander. He went directly to his son's mother's job at lunch.

She was surprised he had come. She had not known he was there even though she knew when he got the news of his son he would be there.

So dropped any breath she might have breathed until her tongue left his mouth. He knew what was next. He still bothered not to stop her slap.

The third godfather stood up and walked directly to them. You came here to kill me too. I know you knew I would come. Before it starts I think you should know. Your boy should have been treated worse that what we gave him.

Your boy raped these one hundred one children. He sodomized them all. Male and female. Here are their mothers in some cases addresses their names and ages, from three years old to twelve years old. In a couple cases their mothers and fathers lived together. Same age group. That is what it has all been about. You murdered two heroes you dumb fuck I wanted you to see my face when I told you. I will be here in case you still want to finish your illness. Your revenge.

Then seven men stood up in the lunchroom and walked to godfather number three, stood beside and the eight started to depart together.

Public or no public the Lakotan's squad members, Tiger Li Jung, stopped it all as they entered together. The war ended when he called them. It's over he said.

No more has been heard since. Two days later three South American drug lords surrounded by hundreds of armed soldiers, in three different camps committed suicide by hanging.

A day later Tiger Li Jung was back in Washington, DC Celebrating

THE END

UNLESS I GET A WRITERS JOB

UNLESS I GET A WRITER'S JOB

I thought to myself. Write a story on a subject none have ever done. Not so easy a task. I have not written a word nor a letter since I made that choice. This is what I have come up with in four day.

The pressure he levied upon the metropolis in the end proved weighty. For more weighty than its citizens, both governmental and regular voters together were able to bare. Therefore he proved successful, rich on the Nuevo – rich and his skin tone again attained.

The people refused to admit to themselves lending every excuse, every prevarication actually the horde thought the rest of the world's peoples they had deemed plausible.

One man is all the specification existed to bring to their knees one and one half million people consisting of liars, cheats and ground chin draggers.

Scrolling in a downward direction those inappropriate people did their utmost barring his murder which a few of them did attempt unsuccessfully, family, health, a home and legal representation which the local and federal police denied. The two latter departments did not relent into his eventual defeat of them as well.

All their efforts stunted? No. Rather eliminated. His billboard photos adorned ninety countries dedicating his successes to honesty, his and to irrepressive forward against their grain striding.

His non-relenting honesty is what proved their impending doom all the way to their irracible defeat. It was once said to him, had your enemies properly eaten, than they would have died of starvation due to their regurgitation on their words predicting your doom. For surely any nourishment taken would have released itself with their fool fallacies.

When he departed their bindings, social and economical he left them bereft of all but anemia and bodily waste functioning. That which they were gastronomically abundant, the lies, deceits and cheatings which their hopes lied on having the planet catch its fires were exposed as on the verge of tyrannical burdens, thus lyrics were befuddled and globally shunned as were they.

The smiles on their deceitful visages were reversed more accurately, upside down. Boy he turned then inside out.

He looked to God instinctively and on this occasion his looks were answered in heavenly favor, on his good stead instead of a positive answer to their evil callings to him who is not evil.

That one action alone tells of how high their stupidity was seen.

His ordeal that he looked back on the most were those months when he carried two to three thousand dollars daily in his front pocket, debit cards with thousands of dollars more on them in his bank accounts, a two carat diamond and ten carat gold ring on his finger but only three pairs of trousers had him believing (somewhat) that clothing manufacturers were against him for no trousers were found for sale in that province size forty six waist. His size.

The one thing that kept him in frame of mind within the region of sanity is that it was during the COVID NINETEEN pandemic, so he chose to address the situational problem on supply could not get to him. Maybe his creator used that to strengthen him. If so he though, my mouth is wide figuratively wide open, please feed me!!!

One city conquered two more to go. Next up Trenton in New Jersey. Fifteen days in the future. Still there was work to do. This should be the easiest of the three. Its loss if right is to prevail lies on one answer. A subpoena he believes the opponent has no right not to answer but he is quite sure that knowing their loss is in the order that they will make the move not to surrender it. He knows it will most likely take a second order by the magistrate. The law is on his side. Well they should know it. Still he is leory of the legal system. He is no stranger to its shadiness and its ways of cloaking truth to envoke that of which is in its sinewy vile heart along with its unyielding other organs unless forced into honesty.

His motto, Justice is not blind unless your back it turned towards the Shehe's direction. Then male, female or born with both male and female genitals, watch out.

It had not taken him good long years in life to realize that truth, though he had himself disgusted himself. He had never seen a dual sexual organed one. Not that he knew. Therefore placing a hermaphrodite into that scenario without knowledge of how a dual sexual would react facing justice or not facing the Shehe, he should not draw a staunch conclusion. Perhaps, they as a whole even had different personalities and it may even be possible would react differently to a like stimulus.

Ignorance. Damn that part.

Hatred embroiled within his almost total being. "That part".

He knew what he had blocked. His full awareness precluded him from not realizing. Ignorant being part of the defition. Still he fought. The round was automatic with him. He knew the holding it back from himself would mark a one higher in his column of loses.

The glance he took towards the door followed by the shortly timed stare on the Persian throw rug he stood on.

The loosing was creeping into his brain, thought into him.

That glance did not kick out to the curb outside of the building where he had entrusted his presence. It's coming. If the glance had I oh it not I would be awaiting me in an ambush along the trek. "Nigger"

While dreaming of delaying it forever if not forever than for a long gestating period caused the collapse of his guard. His defenses had been not only breached but done so quickly.

He also tried to disguise the disaster. Purposely the past image of himself in the construction sites port-o-potty. She was the distraction he smoothly put in place of his ignorance. The biggest vaginal opening he had seen in his sixty years of life. Her two inside lips, are they also called lips? The inside pair attached to the outside pair next to her thighs. He could have put a baseball right in them with no stretch at all.

Ha ha. Fooled you. I bet you thought a few moments would go by before I did start to write again. Well if you did, you were wrong. --- This time.

I know you are not trying to check out my past! Hunh?! Good.

I do have one question for you. Do you feel uncomfortable those times I checked out yours? Since I may not like your answer, I can't the question. It is can't rather than recan't? Is it? If not can't rather than recan't, since it is only once it should be.

If I can find her again, he thought. Her, "I thought you liked me" on occasion reigned havoc on his find.

He thought I have got to learn how to take one home with me. She would run through his memory again at those times too. The word cavernous echoed in his eventually regretful relenting.

Maybe, just maybe that one was a loss looking at his images, his facial reflection his smile came to an abrupt end again. Why? Why does this so-called most medically advanced country not order? It's military veterans dentures from a company whose oral appliances are not a brilliant white in the stead of these off yellows? This bothersome inquiry annoyed him to the brink of utmost.

Oh well. Also maybe not. Perhaps when his guns healed well enough from the last extractions of eleven molars, his replacements to the dentures, his upcoming permanent implants may came from a factory where gleaming whites are the norm, a disheartening hmm came from his sounding esophagus through the somewhat flared due to the memory of the dentures nostrils.

The walk over to their did not take long. Seven minutes. He arrived one hour from the time that he left to go there.

On his way he had to cross Berks Boolevard West. On the south west corner was the Austria Citizens savings and Loan.

The billboard above was electronic. A skinny bolemic blonde teen girl a prototype of the influx of bolemic models to soon show up all over city advertising a new weight gain pill that guaranteed a protein built body. No fat.

It was the ladder behind the sign that grabbed at his attention. Only the banks chain link fence hindered access. He and an oversized hooker made that blockage easy as a footstool and ascended the ladder to the sign. Her shorts now off revealed her hair that would have made a bald headed man proud.

She must have been clean there. He had no odor; no sign of a scent was on him when he met his wife for star watching. She however was not as choicey nor as uncented. The memory kept to an irregular relentless faked mewing, moaning and jerking's. He would of it times concede to the temptation of mounting her but his images of her faking it with whoever jaunted into him time he touched her with the angst of having sex with her. His visions seemed real to him. Her tongue barely excepting his with even the mearest of caring to have it.

On rare occasion has she given her husband the treatment she gave to the men she left a mere hour ago.

There she was with Bob Hopkins about to do her thing. He went to work at the start on her vulva. A few seconds on she released her first drop of lemony colored pee. The second drop came a few seconds after the first. That was when she also cut the cheese. As he got together with his proud bearing she seduced him. Sssst, oh, shortly pausing while awaiting his reaction hoping he would be reeled in and continue his tongue lathering. Uhh, Uhh, mmm. Lick, lick, lick move to another spot between the middle of her urine hole and clit. A short, short small stream right down his throat. An oh God, was murmered. As he paid the faked gleeful outery she raised her lips in another of those faked jerks. A quiet expurgation directly into his open mouth and then came the false pre orgasm. She woman handled the sides of his face and wrapped her legs tightly over his shoulders. A couple seconds later just before flopping herself back down on the throw rug on. The linoleum covered floor a couple of pumps to his face and as the head and female torso were delivering themselves to the throw rug a ssssst came into mouth and nose. Only the "t" part was audible to his ears.

After that she gave him some pussy and sucked his asshole anyway. He tried his damnedest to cut one loose, but it wasn't in him. Her mouth still stunk because he really, really needed to do better at cleansing his anus.

She went onto Harry's and then to Heriberto's. The same actions took place. Only Heriberto did cleans himself more with tounge and her lips than he had ever done in the shower. When Heriberto left his gas in her wide open mouth, something came out along with the gaseous excursion.

When she reached her husband, she really stank. Her rancor showed his no respect. Which is exactly what he deserved.

The falling star shower over they began the quiet walk home. She did not reach for hand the whole trip.

She thought only to French kiss him. A long, juicy mouth slobbering dripping down his throat one.

It was eighty six degrees. Clear as a bell. The two begin the slightest quivering. A small chill. The two began to feel nervous. Something definitely was ascue. What in the fuck was it. What was going on. A second ago the most pricey apartment in the business district were surrounding them on both side of the way. All of a sudden it was cool, dark and he was alone lying on what appeared to be a metal table, he once gathered, almost anyway tried to move to get to a sitting position. The eye looking into his split open body as though being dissected kept him still.

Pieces of him were pulled out one by one. Pieces of him were put back, but not all of them. A part was held. No way in any of the human languages could describe what is was that held that part. The part went away. A similar part to the one that went away appeared inside his body where the first piece has been pulled from.

He was found the next morning as the sun was dawning. The police were putting him in the back of a van. He was coming into a conscious state. He still could not move on his own.

As his full awareness came his nakedness came into his eyes view. There was a hard face, hefty bag of a female cop closing the back door. He meant to cover his embarrassment. He was not built very well down there, so he tried to cover it.

Realizing she must have already seen it as he hands would not do the job they were asked to do. The hands cuffs.

All sort of jokers and complements went through his head hoping to defer her vision at his smallness in manhood.

Sitting there as he was he wanted to cuss her. She kept peeping into the van via the small window. He could not cover physically so he chose bravado, thrusting his exposed crotch towards the window. Something smacked his sight with a sled hammer's weight in his awakening. His cock was massive. He blinked. Then he blinked at it. It was huge. A foot long maybe- hanging down, limp. He chose not to blink again as blinking again had occurred to him. His balls were thick and- daamnn, big. No more damned blinking, he thought. One eye closed. Shut tight. The other widened open looking downward. Now he remembered. The opened body. The new piece put inside of him. That is when he got it all. That body part on his inside was not the only thing the eye had replaced. In this space ease inserts the little.

ALIEN ABDUCTION

Tap, Tap came an almost silent noise on the van door. It was her. The cop. Pointing into his newest member. Sure she had his attention she looked left and then she looked right, back towards him she pointed to his family member, blew it kiss with a licking tongue motion. He eyes and mind were aroused to a point. One he had never had before. The van pulled off on its way to the precinct.

The speckled horsefly hit by the sudden rush of winds as the police van pulled away lifted into wind skyward and with its horsefly buzzing its nagging sound flew away. None took notice of the flight of such a small being. The goings on took president demanding the areas full attention. Every spectator was in their various appearances of gawks, smirks, laughings, whispers if dismay. The insect completely extinct for over twenty years went unseen.

The sun now fully in the sky two policeman get the security code correct and enter the rear door with almost naked prisoner, only a grey military tempory emergency blanket covering him. The sort of chubby police woman who had aroused his memory of her while being transported to jail was left behind by her commands- in - arms to lend her hand should crimes rise its ugly head. Her memory had it at three quarter staff poking between ends of the blanket.

Moses Frazier Pearson had been assigned the duty of receiving incoming detainees. The television already had the audio set on ten of one hundred. The beep went off. He checked the rear doors camera screen. Press access. His job done officer Milosh Mirales took the prisoner to an unoccupied cell. No need to search him nor did there exist the need to take his personal effects, shoe strings and belt.

He came backwards in time to a memory a year ago when a female came in as did this prisoner. He remembered her torso hair must never ever have been shaven also never trimmed. He remembered movie about the jungles in South America. He also remembered at that time the jungle in the movie looked bereft next the sight of that woman, Murriell McCarroll Williams's pussy hairs.

Walking escorted to an empty cell the determine heard on the T.V. today, Elio Muskatello, announces he has successfully built the first space craft to land on Jupiter. The trip is to last three years. The purpose of the trip, actually three trips is to colonizer the micro planet for future generations to live. He further stated that six months after the first landing six hundred miles will have livable quarters life sustaining buildings sufficient to house four thousand occupants and workers. The first flight will be two weeks from today. Taking on that trip will be over a thousand builders with building equipment and armed security forces.

He did not here the rest. Boy have they got some surprises waiting for them he said to his jailer, as the key turns, and locks him in.

The wrapping paper came to him neatly folded. In the were two slices of white sandwich bread. The bread on two slides of a cold scrambles egg came along presented to him by another uniform wearer coupled with a waxed corrugated sealed four ounce carton of Blain brand tea with lemon.

He had not thought to ask for sustenance. It put him to sleep.

The dream of the police woman came along quietly with a message. The two were there together in the precinct's prisoner cell area. She in the next him. Him listening to her. Still nude and still hung gloriously well. Ok. You have a deal. He said to her while lying on an uncomfortable steel bench attached to the wall in his cell.

A shake of her chubby head up and down and out came the words. Me and my girls, her group of crooks, not her children steal cars. We take them to our garages and strip them of a driver tags, serial numbers and windshield stickers. We toss ownership and insurance papers in the shreader. Then we put new stickers, license tags, serial identification and new ownership papers. We do a damned good job of it too. You plate them he said. Yeah.

Then we insure them, crash them up. In less than three months over hundred grand insurance settlement for being in the crash. It's a good start. We good? She asked.

He stood walked to the bars holding the two in separate cage- line rooms complete with toilets. She comes to the bars looks up at him into his eyes. He realizes she is shorter than he had imagined. Cry scene up next.

He is known by all he is acquainted, a man who keeps his word after he had given it.

Beginning to pay his debt his pointed finger beckons she do a one eighty. His flat palm on her thoracic back bone, he guides is to bend. She surprises him with her agility, her palms flat on the jail room floor.

He has a bit of difficulty with their heights matching. He can only penetrate her anus about ten of his thirteen and a quarter stiff. Even almost four inches short of him she has pressed the floor hard so as not to fill away from the in and out pound, pound, pound, pound fully in and then an inch or in to fully in pound, pound, pound to an inch or so out. Two minutes later as tight as she is he gets the call. The alarm goes off. Its almost time. If you want to go on you had better slow your pace. No go. He is about, but he awakens. Naked and alone on that uncomfortable steel jail cell room bench.

His eyes open for a second or two but his imaginary silhouette argues with his awakened self and unsuccessfully he was back in dreams world. If you think leaders are smart enough you can. Substitutive he's for he was.

Steel like room of a sort held him. There he felt odd. The oddity of being himself but also someone else. He really did not know, but if he had an idea the same thing would have happened, the eye. He woke. Still naked. Still in a jail cell. Still lying on his side on that steel bench facing the wall. Still naked. He remembering where he was and in what condition his person was in. He turned his back from the door. The locked door. He turned his back to the wall and faced that door.

He was chilly. His dick was cold, so he grabbed the head of it to bring it warmth. It was wet. The sperm was stringy, stretchy. He pulled it into a line. It glinted from the light bulb in the hallway outside the cubicle.

The question in his mind was answered shortly. His thoughts. When I woke up before. Before I turned over. It was her the cop who licked her lips and twirled her pointer finger in the air at me. She had just locked the door. That door. Then she walked off. She. She. Before she waited away she winked at me. He had the definition as to his dummy prick head.

He came so close, but lost it. The reason his but hole had a tenderness, a cold warmth, a little bit of soreness all the way of his-his question loomed on the cuff. His ignorance. What is the name of that thing that emits faces into my, containing himself to stay ignorant, the intestines. Whatever they call it, those educated doctors, and He was sore up to there. He refuse to admit the heat and tender soreness in there. An eye flashed, his coldness shivered copped with defiance. His defiance fending off knowledge. His not wanting to ascertain, may not want to realize forced that defiance to kick knowledge's ass directly to the curb.

The public defender for the others prisoners going to court in this precinct had been passing through giving a call to her clients making sure they were all here and to inform of her name and the name of the other defense lawyer working with today, so he grabbed her attention. Yes she would be representing him. He had only been charged with nudity. Had had been held for nine hours and no other complaints had come in on him, so he would be going home simply by signing his name and agreeing to show up in court to answer his charges. When would he have to return to court? He had questioned her, As soon as is called a date will be set. I will arrange for you to be given a set of clothing to west home in case you can't call anyone. O.K. Thanks I'll be getting on into the courtroom now.

The other public defender had beckoned her. Court was about to start. As Um a Thurs, the public defender he had conversed with mindfully discharged her body headed to the court room, her brain had a fixed picture of herself and the detainee she had just given his status to.

She was raw, mocked, globs of saliva stuck to her chin extending from the corners of her mouth. She spread eagled only head, arms and calves in view. The detainee had covered the rest of her from knees to neck. His head aside hers, but there was a peek of her nipple being pressed to he side and a stupid looking eyes wide open glassy and satisfied stupid look on her face.

The clothing come presented to him by Officer Melvin Blane. He wore briefs but only boxers were given him. The trousers were thirty eight waists, He wore thirty fours, but the belt took care of that problem.

Buttoning his shirt, a short sleeved Howairen style, mostly blue.

He wondered if they also had remotes clothing. Decided in on ascue way that it made no difference for when men and women are in a gathering it is correct and appropriate to refer to the group to the group as masculine.

Where that thought came from, even he did not know.

His wire was not with him. When he came to and was summerly arrested for being naked and indecently exposed. That bump she had gotten on her used to be flat ass had a new way of life to come. That little bump was about to get the shit fucked out of it. He had come to forms with the fact that he and she had been abducted. He had to the proof was right there hanging down the inside of his left thigh, all the down to his knee.

He also had to force his mind that the whole of his intestines hurt. That he had been probed anally op-papes.

It would not matter, he had a huge schlong, Thank you, you bastards, never would he ask, why.

In Hemoboken Chile, Tabernadle Nemoy lights up when. She gets a telephone call Lois Aber Jongus the Chilean Minister of Metaphysical Funds Dispersment.

A grant of one hundred billion, two hundred million CLP's, Chilean Peso's, to study and find what the average number of married women have regular anal sex with their own husband compared to the times that same couple having sex without their togetherness being anal.

Scientifically that study would show brilliantly how Chile married popular can grow in the future.

Nemoy brought the idea of the study home with her from the North American continent. She thought it an oddity Philadelphia, Mississippians chose anal sex as an antidote to cheating spouses. Bott sex was to be an apologetic response to their male mates once the infeldelous wife's returned home. Some other used anal appreciation as freak way to have sex. She had found many of those had freak sex very often. On her own account when she was with a single partner, if she was in the mood she would participate.

Her problem was she never had a stiff one anywhere in her pores a stiff one longer the five inches, even as a young child of two years old she always seemed to get the tiny too dick guys.

She became aware she was not alone now. Starting to ease towards her handed down from her mother's world war two child rapist sergeant William Sheoftz when they met decades later in Peru the fully loaded, fully functional mauser P08 Luger.

As her body went to turn towards the pillow on the sofa she kept that one behind. It was the weapon closes to her standing position. Her hand tried with a moment of great effort to release the hold her middle and forefinger. Her clitoris could not become free of them. She feared. The living room only a nanosecond later held her presence no more.

She knew what had happened. There were few like her. When taken they realized there leaving. Even fewer still came to them knowing their leaving their trip on the way and are aware at the arrival. She was not a fewer.

When her eyes again opened her legs were wet, her feet too were wet. She with an uncommon instinct touched herself. Yes. She had peed herself. Why? This had not happened since early childhood.

She was sore. Her throat raw. As she moved she knew. She thought she knew. She had been raped.

She walked back in her house. She was pretty good with being careful. She did not cut her arm or hand while breaking the small window pane in her kitchen door. No scratches or cots when she reached inside to unlock it. No cutting the bottom of her feet, not even when she picked up the glass with the broom and long handled dust pain. She vacuumed the smallest of the unseen frags. Place tape with waxed paper over the opening and called, Houdini, the locksmiths that drive the Hummer trucks.

She had the types of looks on all her exterior doors without keys you could not lock them nor could the locks be unlocked without a key.

When Houdini arrived to repair the window she had to get her door key from her bedroom out of her pocket book. Light! How in hell did I get outside?

That nagged her. When Bob the Houdini guy left she checked her wardrobe for when she awakened in her back yard she was naked. She checked her wardrobe. Nothing missing except the evening bag she loaned to, Jethro. His daughter loved that beg, so that loan was put in his care for the child's show at school.

That too accounted for, why would I go out nude? And again how the hell did I get outside without my door key?

Normally by this time of day that button between her lower lips would be getting vibrated and massaged. She had a real need for that sort of attention. More than most. She felt odd. She felt strange. Not the super hero strange came to her mind. A loving smile though short lived came across both her thought and small lips. Breten, that grandson of hers and his action figures. White haired baby boy. You gotta love him. The little scamp. She felt unnatural for her. The feeling was lasting. She had came to in the yard over seven years ago. No sexual urges grabbed at her. She felt fulfilled? So odd was that feeling, it came to her as both an answer and that answer was glammed as a question.

Two days before she had her checkup. Labs came back four days later and her doctors secretary called her cell number. We need you to come into the office. Your labs show your T-Cell count is three eighty. Doctor Medvo says he can have your prescriptions sent to your favorite pharmacy or if you choose you can come to the office and pick them up. My T-Cells? Yes a low count shows you have contracted HIV, the virus that can lead to you getting AIDS.

Oh, shit. Finally it happened, she said quietly. Lock I'm coming in there today. This evening I want you to recheck. See you at six. The phones both hung up.

Baked chicken was good. Steamed rice, asparagus, and glazed carrots filled her hunger. She could now check her stomach as full. Out the door to the doctors.

In the circle she lived in a neighbors hand slaps her butt. She lets him out of her arms and goes on her weary feeling way. There was a time that slap would have juiced her up and a quick quickie would immediately follow. She still felt sexually unaroused. Not even an expression of damn come to her as did on those few and far between occasions when she was to pressed to take a quick suck of a quick ass licking. She was not only good at it too, she was exceptional. It made her whole body stiff sucking on pair of buttocks and anus. Her stimulations did not cause her to even gave that a second of consideration.

One wonders why not if one had been in her acquaintances. One face could be washed with vaginal orgasmic fluids when doing her anus orally.

Sun was about to go down when she left her driveway. Pressing the security button on her steering column the gate slid to the left. The gate has been remaintained. Her taking notice of that? If aloud, one would ask of her, who are you?

Her only conversations were wine, money and how fucking positions are we going to do? No matter the number you came up with, there were not enough for her.

I'm not taking this whatever vere until my now test come back. You want the results in the morning? I have a boo who works for the bio- tech firm we have doing our work. For a little geeche I'll got her to do it tonight. Geeche? A little dow. How little? Two, three hundred. Two fifty. I am sure that will do. Call me then.

On her way out the doctor's secretary walks her to the door.

The call came to the doctors office early. I did these test three times. The analysis verifies both samples came from the same DNA, but the last sample from last night has no sign of T-Cell degradation. This isn't possible. So she has no HIV? Not now, but she did according to her first test. Look I had my supervisor check and says report the first samples results to the Board of Health, so that I have to do. So what do I tell our patient? Everything I guess.

The two hung up after confirming tonight's meeting. Why they always bothered to confirm is even beyond their own understanding. For the last six months they have not had a night away from each other. That they both knew. What the secretary knew the lab technicians did not is the secretary was due to the patient was two hundred fifty dollars richer.

Merelyn Chambers the severely autistic thespian has turned up after being reported missing from mansion last night. It is still unknown weather she was taken from her home. No kidnappers were reported to have contacted her family, therefore no ransom was reported being asked for or paid. It is reported she though autistic is in excellent health.

The mansion is one of the most highly secured building as one all billion aires homes.

You need to tell me where you were me. The houses security is in need of a major upgrade, please tell me? No way mother M, the cameras you were on show you eating a pheasant drumstick and you shock like you about to seiaunes. Mother I do not suffer but you disappeared while the camera was running. Lo Biondo, the security chief went over the tope. What he said was what happened was on impossibility. On three cameras you just vanished from one frame to the next. I am fine mom. Then where in God's name were you? What

The what is as far as Lembetti chambers could get to ask of her question to her daughter. A finger from Marilyn's hand touched the mothers lips to silence. I am fine mom. I am better now than I have ever been.

Present at that conversation were the Chamber's cook, upstairs and downstairs maid and the head of the Chamber's house staff Signed Olsten the butler who witnessed the priest part of this seemingly miracle.

Marilyn Chambers was so autistic she could not hold a conversation not a thought for more than five minutes. The Marilyn Chambers that stood there before them had returned to her form of two years ago. She was articulate. She was quite attentive to conversation and remembered the servants positions and names correctly. She stood there then beconed Sigried leave. She got naked and told Letta Hildergrate, the upstairs maid lay out fresh adornment and those gigglies thirty four b.s bounced and swayed left, right, left, right to the shower room.

Mrs. Chambers sat there in an amazed awe her mouth now shut tight. When she saw her daughter ass larger than it should have been, who to hold responsible. Her amazement was not amused. Now that that had come to light, Marilyn, her daughter had lips that seemed different, large, fuller and wider than before the illness had taken control of her life.

She and her daughter would talk later. Not girl to girl this time. Mother avenging mother to her oldest child. There soon would be hell-to – pay. Still her quietness kept control of a roaring volcano soon to be unleashed on those who dishonored her home.

In the shower she had soap ail over her face, ears, and neck. More soap on her evenly sized shoulders, her back, arms and breasts. Her abdomen who had a thick layer of bubbly suds. Her beautiful thick legs were also slippery with bubbles all the way from her hips down to hand over her well manicured polished toes. The only the place the soap was not is where her fingers kept going in and out of. Still it was very slippery.

When she came from the shower a large beath towel wrapped around her now concealed body.

Her mother held the servants in her bedroom looking for clue to vent her rage. She needed no clue. Her daughter walked up to Letta Hildergrath, whom had the night clothing out laying on the posturpedie double thick matters silk sheets showing a print of white lilacs on a hill of clover and with lightning quickness and Mike Tyson strength knock out the maid. Perfect left roundhouse to temporo mandibular jaw joint.

The physical assault on the housekeeper is how I got into this. The senior most Mrs. Chambers mother Ludritia Mass, called to handle any legal claim the housekeeper may bring to civil trial.

I love the Ludritia. She explained the happenstance to me. How do you want me to handle it Hotstuff? I asked her over the phone.

I was on my REVLL flip down cell. She was on her bad chamber Federal Antique Desk Phone, white with gold colored trimming.

Not even one cent. She said to me calmly. In that manner and that slow direct wording I know what she had said is in compliance to exactly what she meant and would adhere to I do love that Ludiritia.

The tone of that was purely musical. Music to my ears, mind, heart and brain. I dooo love tat Ludiritia.

Before I continue on that latest of occurrences, it is felt by me a necessity to give you my background with the chambers family.

When I was seven years old. I had to go on the lam. I put an end to my foster father's child molesting by taking the blunt end of his axe to the upper part of his spinal trail. I hit him as hard as I could. He had no idea what was coming. He crumpled first to his knee and then crumlike writing on the floor. Turning the handle until the sharp aligned with my next intention I severed his his head and neck from his shoulders.

I was caught a couple weeks later and was charged and given a trial date. In jovey hall awaiting my guilty verdict two guys one twelve and one fifteen came to the same notion of my mouth and backside as had did my late stepfather.

What I did to the fifteen year old was not what the judge order me into the state of Iowa, Blendell City Psychiatric Hospital- Children's Wing for.

Stabling that punk ass bastard in his eye with a five inch long shard of broken glass introducing an inch or two of it into his brain showed no sign of me being mentally unstable only homicidal.

Calling his croany into my cubicle and gutting him after slicing his throat is why the doe sent me there.

The security there was better. No chance of a pubertious homosexual rape event. The youth study center, youth prison, in actuality was same from my hetero interuptus murderous influence.

I met a female firebug there. She was sixteen years old and me now eleven.

Discussing our cases with other inmates was strictly a no-no, but Blythe Danner Mass had a way with a guard and got the lowdown on everyone she came into contact with.

That is how I found out that being a hetero had some good points. He tongue and vagina did wonders for my loneliness.

Later the night before she was to be picked until she turned twenty-one a male intern called her from the dinner hall. I saw him push her into a toilet area.

His neck gushed from both arteries. You have been told of them one way or another. She went onto jail.

He family lawyer came to see me. Six days later I was in pre-college classes. Charges of homicide were never followed through with.

That's my background on how I got to be on the Mass's payroll and doing so attained two master's degrees.

Blythe Danner Mass and Marilyn Chambers are twin sisters. Blythe the oldest by twelve minutes.

I'll mention this. It really has no effect on the story other than to show why the twins carry different last names.

I met Marilyn's husband Joseph Bazouka Chambers once. Only once before he went missing a few years back. Biggest son- of- a bitch I ever seen. Over six ten and pushed six hundred. Nice guy, he had the clout. He summed me to meet him in Hawaii. I flew over in the yellow family twelve seater.

He and I met as he ordered at Diamond Head. We talked for hours. This and that. Socialities and business, both of us standing stop and looking down into the almost inert volcano. The next year he apparently from the face of earth disappeared.

I watched the footage of over three dozen attacks on Marilyn by the house's upstairs maid while the heiress's medical condition was still ongoing. How the autism all of a sudden stopped may need to be looked into.

Marilyn had been strap- on dildo raped more than a hundred times. She was ridden as though the two were husband and wife. There was no doubt of it. No breakings, no thefts, so no reason to view the security footage. Not until Marilyn disappeared into thin air. The one thing is the maid was a servant in that house for fifteen years.

I talken to Marilyn. I had a feeling I thought I knew the answer. How would like me to handle this M? I asked. I want her to suffer the same way she made me, but with spiked one. One for one.

Okay. I said. That is how you would handle it, but what do you want me to do. Keep me out of jail.

I like M, too.

M, I asked, thinking I would not want to know her answer, can you remember anything about where you were. She hid it from me. No.

I remember M, from before the illness struck her. When she gave a one word answer you might as well open an empty oyster. You were going to get nothing from her. I like M. Almost as much as I like Ludruitia.

Both were common in looks but well stacked and in personal care they both were immaculate. Pearlie white gleaners too. Some wealthy folk these days were turning yellow there.

Okay kiddo. I exited. Got to the outside walkway and exited. Inside the house in peoples presence would have been unwelcomed and gauche.

I called Doctor Adam Arkin as he was about to get in his Mazzerati Eplanix. We been on good standings since he did not inpune my anus and still diagnosed my pendistist.

I know what you're going to ask. I have no idea how but she is cured. He got in his car buzzed the guard of the gate and gave him the word. He now could exist without incident.

I'm happy. Doe's got a good marriage. When Mrs. Mass enlisted me to investigate his wife's filandering. I found her straight forward, an honest wife and wonderful mother. I can almost understand the rumors and inuendos of her fooling around. She was of the physical attributes of the likes of Jane Mansfield and a Marilyn Monroe.

The woman was also a brilliant scientist and business woman. Doe did not have to work but what he did he loved and it kept him from getting into any trouble.

The doctor gone. My talk with Marilyn complete what Ladritia asked me to do all but sewn up. I took the time, only a couple moments really to look downward at the lawn but in my mind seething the outer space on the other side of the planet. I too took look upwards towards the sky on this side of the planet. Admittedly I did not look left nor did I look right. It did not occur to me at that time. The recorded film of M vanishing could not give to dispute. Yes I want to believe. M was cured in one night. Our medicals could not dare to dream she could be cured. Yes, I believe. I like M. Still looking outer space ward, thank you.

Three days later. Headlines and news outlets read, housekeeper of billionaire Chambers found dead on Pea block Beach, viciously raped and decapitated.

The report went on but the little incidentals really matter not, so no writing need be done. Somewhere along the investigation about a week in a letter came to WKBW's newspapers division. The senior editor owned Flabbergasted the third highest selling glamour magazine. Flabbergasted was making inroads into Columbia, South America and also in the four Canadian provinces.

The video of a billionaires disappearing into thin and returning within twenty four four hours cured of her disease she had been suffering from for almost five years with no progress in sight by the best physicists, psychologist and neuro specialist on this planet. Other than the first word in the expose being capitalized as was journalistic norm the only other capitalized words written in the article were "On This Planet".

Ludritia Mass, gave me a call. She had not read the remainder of the story. The part about how a Russian Taylor / seam stress who ran her own business was being filmed with her new designs for boys shirts and girls dresses disappeared into thin air, returned the next morning fully capable of talking and understanding all the languages of Canada and the language of Columbia, South America and American English who had never spoke or understood any languages other than Russian and Ukranian.

Nor did she read about the boy who had stomach acid splashed into his eyes when his father murdered his mother ripping her guts out with a butcher's knife. He had been blind since the age of two. He went missing from his bed at night. Returned on his front door stairs early the next evening. No cameras from the neighborhood business saw him approach his apartment home. His sight fully restored with no sign of any burns and no scarring.

When she called me. I took the call when I saw he number. I cautioned the thousand dollars an hour hooked not to stop. So sue me I like my ass being licked, sucked and kissed. To keep it clean, I like my ass kissed in many ways.

When Ludritia calls, it is my turn to do the ass kissing.

As far as the best way to get an ass kissed I have had some number of dreams of me being with her. Did I mention she has small delicious looking lips. One day Ludritia Mass.

That day came sooner than I thought. I read the full story. Ludritia went to work. She has a great brain. It is probably the thing stronger than her clout.

Two months later on the flight to Guebee to meet the Russian busy woman, the newly sighted boy to muddle the Russian wear and the magazine owner. Ludritia set it all up perfectly.

The motherly tits were suptly bouncey. No sagging, all creamy with no difference in color of those thimble sized nipples. Without feelings them they were unseeable. My salvia now drying on them and in my mouth. The purple fingerprints on them came from my hands squeezing them so many times about twenty sets of hands.

Her legs wrapped down on my upper back and shoulders were turning blue. Her veins pushed outward. The gasps she been doing for hours came from the ten times I had come in the thick still blue ass and darkening purple asshole. My dick could not get soft. Twenty four times I had cum in her. The last two only a drop or so. She had me hard as ban aluminum soft ball bat but it was spunt, incapable of movement. She slide out from under me and mounted my back. Those spasms could have caused that mountain in Howai to erupt. She had her head facing my backside. Her two hands parted my ass crack. I felt her breath in my hole, her lips made a smacking noise. A noise of the pure musical ecstasy that was about to start. I knew then her tongue was about to enter or rim my asshole.

Sir. Sir! Sir!! Wake up. We are here. Jessica is the private orange jet on board hostess. I saw her as my eyes gave birth to reality. Remind me one day to eviscerate Jessica.

My notes were complete before I fell into dream nightmare land. I remembered one thing as I grabbed the umbrella for that long four or five feet trip to the limo outside the jet. I had talked in my sleep. Jessica?

Jessica Shirnna, was no super good looking female. She was only a step or two above the realm of entering into looking plain.

I have flown with her over the years no less than ten times and never has her expression on her visage revised.

Before going through the door I said to her since we were on good terms, Jess, I said, Yes sir? Remind me to viscerate you. Still no revampment in expression. I went to press the up bottom on my London Fog umbrella. It up and down the metal stairs I go.

Jessica Shirnna, gave a bread jubilant grin.

As he departed the jets stairs to the yellow limo Jessica's mind had replaced Ludritia. She headed to the front of the jet and got on the pillow on the cabin floor between the pilot and the co-pilot and unseen from the landing run away pursued her hobby.

The limosine's occupants never heard the expletive phrase. It could not be heard over the screaming shriek. Their surprise was defined in the above.

Jessica on every flight waited until VIP's left the jet and began giving oral on the pilot and did not touch the co-pilot and did not touch the co-pilot until she had swallowed all the pilot's jism. This moment or two after pilot's cock was fully covered by her mouth the pilot disappeared into thin air. The limo was on its way.

Printed in the United States
by Baker & Taylor Publisher Services